NEW YORK REVIEW BOOKS
CLASSICS

WALKABOUT

JAMES VANCE MARSHALL is the pseudonym of Donald Payne
(b. 1924). Only half a dozen Marshall novels have appeared in the last
fifty years but they have sold several million copies and been translated
into seventeen languages. Two, including *Walkabout*, have been made
into films.

Walkabout is a work of collaboration between Donald Payne and
the Australian James Vance Marshall (1887–1964). Marshall spent
much of his life in the outback of Australia—a part of the world he
knew intimately and loved deeply. He wrote a series of articles about
the people, flora, and fauna of the outback, and with his permission,
Payne used these articles as background for their novel *Walkabout*.

Subsequently, and with the consent of Marshall's son, Payne
continued to publish under the pseudonym Marshall; his most recent
book is *Stories from the Billabong* (2008), a collection of Aboriginal
legends retold as stories for children.

LEE SIEGEL is the author of four books, including *Against the
Machine: How the Web Is Reshaping Culture and Commerce—and
Why It Matters* and *Are You Serious: How to Be True and Get Real in
the Age of Silly*. He has written essays and reviews for many publica-
tions, including *Harper's Magazine*, *The New Republic*, *The Atlantic
Monthly*, and *The New York Times*. In 2002, he received the National
Magazine Award for Reviews and Criticism.

WALKABOUT

JAMES VANCE MARSHALL

Introduction by
LEE SIEGEL

NEW YORK REVIEW BOOKS

New York

THIS IS A NEW YORK REVIEW BOOK
PUBLISHED BY THE NEW YORK REVIEW OF BOOKS
435 Hudson Street, New York, NY 10014
www.nyrb.com

Library of Congress Cataloging-in-Publication Data
Marshall, James Vance, 1924–
Walkabout / by James Vance Marshall ; introduction by Lee Siegel.
    p. cm.
ISBN 978-1-59017-490-6 (alk. paper)
1. Airplane crash survival—Fiction. 2. Children—Fiction.
3. Australia—Fiction. I. Title.
PR6066.A9W35 2012
823'.914—dc23
                    2011043823

ISBN 978-1-59017-490-6

Printed in the United States of America on acid-free paper.
10 9 8 7 6 5 4 3 2 1

can one escape the elemental reality of destruction. What is left for the girl is a lie about life, which will protect her against the lie of her existence even as it makes it easier for her to live out her self-deceit. If the Aborigine boy's spirit survives at all, if she is able to recall him as a pure soul incapable of lying, it is only because he killed himself—an honest self-obliteration that is contrasted with the father's demented self-destruction. For Roeg, only violence and death do not lie. It is the glamorous apocalypticism of a director who made one of his next movies with David Bowie.

"It was silent and dark, and the children were afraid." That is how the novel begins. With the cadences of the First Story, we are transported to the primacy of storytelling: "And the earth was without form, and void; and darkness was upon the face of the deep."

James Vance Marshall's *Walkabout*—the London-born author's real name is Donald Gordon Payne—resembles reflective fictions like Marjorie Kinnan Rawlings's *The Yearling* or John Steinbeck's *The Red Pony*, Indeed, the book's original title was *The Children*. The story is about children, and it is meant to be read by the eternal child that is the greenest part of the adult mind. If innocence is tested here, it is not condemned as a naïve illusion.

In the novel the two children find themselves alone in the Australian wilderness when the plane they are taking from Charleston, South Carolina, to Adelaide crashes. On the brink of exhaustion and starvation, they encounter the

work, about the status of a colleague, about his own pro-
motion, and similar mundane matters. She looks dreamily
away and transports herself into what appears to be a
memory of the "walkabout" in which the three children
are swimming naked in a pool of water replenished by a
gentle waterfall. And yet no such scene has appeared in the
film, nor is it likely to have happened, since in fact she was
terrified of the Aborigine's nakedness. Rather, it seems
that she has turned the complex experience of the walkabout into the type of exotic, idealized innocence that is
the product of a supremely civilized state of mind. As the
film ends, we hear a voice reciting one of A. E. Housman's
most famous poems:

Into my heart an air that kills
    From yon far country blows:
What are those blue remembered hills,
    What spires, what farms are those?

That is the land of lost content,
    I see it shining plain,
The happy highways where I went
    And cannot come again.

Post-Woodstock, post-Manson, Roeg's startling film is
very much of its disillusioned moment, the early 1970s,
when the naïve enthusiasms of love-ins and flower children
have given way to cynicism and despair. The very memory
of such naïveté and innocence is "an air that kills" the dis-
abused spirit. Neither in civilization nor in the wilderness

Now he stops the car. He orders the girl and boy to lay out a picnic, and while they are doing so, he grabs a revolver out of the glove compartment, steps out of the car, and starts shooting at them. The girl pulls her brother behind a large rock. The father continues to shoot, commanding his daughter in a weird, robotic voice to come to him and to "Bring *him* with you!" "Can't waste time!" he says, as he douses the Volkswagen with gasoline and sets it on fire. Stepping back, he puts the gun in his mouth and pulls the trigger. His daughter watches in horrified disbelief as he drops to the ground in a sitting position. As flames engulf the car, he falls onto his back.

It is a scene of stunning violence, and its repercussions are felt throughout the movie. Stranded in the desert, the children are on the verge of dying of thirst and hunger when they come upon an Aborigine boy, who will lead them back to civilization. To ensure the survival of all three of them, he kills various creatures with terrific violence. In the end, out of some mysterious depression that we are meant to associate with encroaching civilization itself—at one point, he encounters a white hunter shooting game with a high-power rifle—the boy, like the children's father, commits suicide. The story, scripted by avant-garde playwright Edward Bond, the British heir to Antonin Artaud's "theater of cruelty," is framed by violence and self-destruction.

In the film's final scenes, however, the girl is not only restored to civilization but grown up and married to a man much like her father. Standing in their boxy apartment and holding his wife in his arms, he talks about his

INTRODUCTION

I T is the fate of certain novels only to become classics after they become movies, and then to be eclipsed by the movie that made them a classic. James Vance Marshall's enchanting short novel *Walkabout* was published in Britain in 1959. Yet it was not until Nicolas Roeg turned it into a film twelve years later that the book acquired an aura of wide renown, despite the fact that relatively few people had read it. This is an ironic enough fate for a work of literature, but in fact the movie is so strikingly different from Marshall's lovely parable as to verge on travesty. It is a brilliant travesty, though, one that adds a curious urgency to the book's very different, apparently old-fashioned pleasures, which, as it turns out, have a good deal to tell us now.

Roeg's film begins with a by now familiar evocation of the rote asphyxiations of modern Western civilization—the monotonous dress of office workers, the synchronized pace of commuters, etc.—until we see one such office worker, still wearing his gray suit, driving his young daughter and son into the Australian desert in a black Volkswagen. The girl is around fourteen, the boy eight or nine. The girl darts a disapproving glance at her father. We can tell that she doesn't trust him, that she's scared.

Aborigine. "*Kurura*," he tells them, a word that they come to construe as meaning "follow me." And so they do.

Part fairy tale, part moral parable, Marshall's short novel reveals its depths on its surface. Writing about the stranded children, he says: "Coddled in babyhood, psychoanalyzed in childhood, nourished on predigested patent foods, provided with continuous push-button entertainment, the basic realities of life were something they'd never had to face." Having neatly summed up the simple cultural and intellectual context of his tale, as simply as if describing some desert fauna, Marshall gets down to what really interests him, the tale itself.

Marshall portrays the white children as alienated from the "basic realities of life." The Aborigine, by contrast, lives amidst them. "He knew what reality was," we are told. The life of the people he belongs to is "unbelievably simple." Marshall goes on: "Their lives were utterly uncomplicated because they were devoted to one purpose, dedicated in their entirety to the waging of one battle: the battle with death ... Keeping him at bay was the Aboriginals' full-time job: the job they'd been doing for twenty thousand years: the job they were good at."

For all the elements of a classic adventure story in *Walkabout*, the adventure is essentially spiritual. The two children are thrust into a situation where the everyday structures of distraction have been peeled away from what they conceal: the brute fact of mortality. Behind the reassuring familiarity of the children's "comfortable home in Charleston, South Carolina," is the old tale of the "scrimmage of appetite," as someone once called it: the ruthless struggle for food, drink, shelter, and health. In the "primeval desolation" of the desert, they will learn that life is bounded and hounded by death.

Primeval storyteller that he is, Marshall is frank about his choice of a wilderness as the proving ground of his two young characters. The girl's name is Mary and the boy's is Peter. They will experience a redemption from their fallen, civilized state in the comfortable South Carolina suburbs, and even a kind of resurrection of the spirit. But what is somewhat daring in Marshall's unpretentious little parable is that the bushboy himself is the Christ figure. His "walkabout" is his own ordeal by temptation. Though the nature of his temptation is never made explicit, it is clear what it is. He can abandon the two white children to die. He can kill them out of fear and tribal hatred. He can ravish the girl. Instead he comes to the conclusion, in the narrator's words, that "unless he looked after them, they would die." The narrator continues: "It was his people's way to accept individuals as they were: to help, not to criticize, the sick, the blind and the maimed." The nameless bushboy is the spirit of love itself.

Readers falling into the book from the movie might at first be put off by what they feel is Marshall's patronizing idealization of the Aborigine boy. It is true that much of what Marshall attributes to Aborigine culture, including the ritual of the walkabout, seems mostly to be his own concoction. Marshall himself appears to lose the thread of his conception of Aborigine life when, less than twenty pages after invoking the Aborigines' compassionate nature, he defines the walkabout as "a selective test which weeded out and exterminated the weaker members of the tribe, and ensured that only the fittest survived to father children."

Marshall may be guilty of romantic excess here and there, yet his idealizations are justified by his unsentimental grasp of social reality. At one point, the bushboy seems about to touch Mary. "The idea of being manhandled by a naked black boy appalled her," Marshall writes, "struck at the root of one of the basic principles of her civilized code. It was terrifying; revolting; obscene. Back in Charleston, it would have got the darkie lynched." Later, when Mary suddenly catches the bushboy looking at her in wonder as she is bathing naked in a pool of water, she gives him such a look of terror that he believes the death-spirit has sentenced him to die. So certain is he of the death spirit's plans for him that he eventually wills himself to die (the ability to die by autosuggestion perhaps being another of Marshall's fanciful versions of Aborigine culture). Mary is his murderer.

Mary, however, is also his vessel. Two years after the forced integration of an American public school in Little Rock, Arkansas, just as the issue of race was starting to ignite a revolution in American life, Marshall is bringing Christianity back to its moral sources. Having, in a sense, killed the bushboy through the spirit of hatred, Mary becomes the instrument by which the boy's spirit of love and forgiveness lives on. For despite knowing that Mary's terrified glance has spelled his doom, the bushboy decides that he will help the children find their way back home. In the process, he teaches Peter to survive by catching fish in Aboriginal fashion—that is to say, he uses a primitive, pre-Christian technique to teach Peter how to become a true Christian: Simon, the fisher of souls. And when the bushboy dies, he does so with his head in Mary's lap, smiling at her gently:

> It was the smile that broke Mary's heart: that last forgiving smile. Before, she had seen only as through a glass darkly, but now she saw face to face. And in that moment of truth all her inbred fears and inhibitions were sponged away, and she saw that the world which she had thought was split in two was one.

Saved by a black savage, the two white children absorb his clement, generous spirit on their way back to civilization. "*Kurura*," says Peter to his sister at the end of the novel, and you feel that he is liberating the true spirit of Christianity from Christianity itself.

There is nothing labored about any of this, partly because it is unobtrusively woven into Marshall's beautiful descriptions of the desert landscape, as if love were as fundamental a part of the physical universe as the elements themselves. Partly, too, Marshall's modestly subversive variation on the Christian myth is simply another version of the necessity of people to care for one another, which is the moral of the greatest children's literature. That theme is there at the very beginning of the book, when Mary remembers seeing the burning plane after the crash and watching "the figure of the Navigating Officer carrying the pilot and clambering out of the wreckage. In the heat of the explosion, he glowed white-hot, disintegrating." The unforgettable scene is a foreshadowing of Mary and Peter's own discovery, in the disintegrating white heat of the desert, that the navigator's selfless act of trying to save the pilot exists beyond the color of one's skin or the place of one's birth.

Roeg's film also opens with a fire, though his retelling of the story takes a wholly different path. To go from the widely known film to the obscure book is to move from a nightmare vision of collective corruption to the timelessness of a simple story about the "basic realities of life." You may find that to go from the film to the book is similar to the experience of Mary and Peter. You will journey from the hub of darkness, as it were, to the heart of light—from the dehumanizing refinements of civilization to the innocent wilderness itself.

—LEE SIEGEL

WALKABOUT

CHAPTER ONE

IT was silent and dark, and the children were afraid. They huddled together, their backs to an outcrop of rock. Far below them, in the bed of the gully, a little stream flowed inland – soon to peter out in the vastness of the Australian desert. Above them the walls of the gully climbed smoothly to a moonless sky.

The little boy nestled more closely against his sister. He was trembling.

She felt for his hand, and held it, very tightly.

'All right, Peter,' she whispered. 'I'm here.'

She felt the tension ebb slowly out of him, the trembling die gradually away. When a boy is only eight a big sister of thirteen can be wonderfully comforting.

'Mary,' he whispered, 'I'm hungry. Let's have something to eat.'

The girl sighed. She felt in the pocket of her frock, and pulled out a paper-covered stick of barley sugar. It was their last one. She broke it, gave him half, and slipped the other half back in her pocket.

'Don't bite,' she whispered. 'Suck.'

Why they were whispering they didn't know. Perhaps because everything was so very silent: like a church. Or was it because they were afraid; afraid of being heard?

5

For a while the only sounds were the distant rippling of water over stone, and the sucking of lips round a diminishing stick of barley sugar. Then the boy started to fidget, moving restlessly from one foot to another. Again the girl reached for his hand.

'Aren't you comfy, Pete?'

'No.'

'What is it?'

'My leg's bleeding again. I can feel the wet.'

She bent down. The handkerchief that she had tied round his thigh was now draped like a recalcitrant garter over his ankle. She refastened it, and they huddled together, holding hands, looking into the powdery blackness of the Australian night.

They could see nothing. They could hear nothing – apart from the lilt of the rivulet – for it was still too early for the stirring of bush life. Later there'd be other sounds; the hoot of the mopoke, the mating howl of the dingo, and the leathery flip-flap-flip of the wings of flying foxes. But now, an hour after sunset, the bush was silent: frighteningly still: full, to the children, of terrors all the greater for being unknown. It was a far cry from here to their comfortable home in Charleston, South Carolina.

The hours meandered past like slow, unhurrying snails. At last the boy's head dropped to his sister's lap. He snuggled closer. His breathing became slower, deeper. He slept.

But the girl didn't sleep; that would never have done; for she had to keep guard. She was the elder. The responsibility was hers. That was the way it had

6

always been, as far back as she could remember. Always she had been the big sister who had stuck plaster on Peter's knees, had taught him to tie his shoe laces, and had taken the lead in their games of Indians and cowboys. Now that they were lost – somewhere in the middle of an unknown continent – the weight of her responsibility was greater than ever. A wave of tenderness welled up inside her. Always she had big-sistered him; now she must mother him as well.

For a while she sat staring into the darkness; the darkness that was warm, thick and almost tangible; soon her mind became utterly blank. The day's events had been too overwhelming; had drawn on her too heavily. The rhythmic beat of the small boy's slumber came to her lullingly now. Gradually her breathing fell in step with his. The whisper of the creek came to her like the croon of a lullaby. Her eyelids drooped and closed, fluttered and closed again. Soon she too was fast asleep.

*

In the darkness beyond the gully, the bush came slowly to life.

A lumbering wombat came creeping out of his ground den. His short stumpy body forced a way through the underscrub; his long food-foraging snout ploughing through the sandy earth in search of his favourite roots. Suddenly he stopped: sniffed: his nostrils dilated. He followed the strange new scent. Soon he came to the gully. He looked the children over; thoughtfully, not hungrily, for he was a vege-

7

tarian, an eater of roots. His curiosity satisfied, he shambled slowly away.

Random fireflies zigzagged by; their nightlights flickering like sparklets from a roving toy-sized forge.

Soon, creeping along the edge of darkness, came another creature: a marsupial tiger-cat, her eyes widened by the night to glowing oriflammes of fire. She too had scented the children; she too clambered into the gully and looked them over. They smelt young and tender and tempting; but they were large; too bulky, she decided, to drag back to her mewling litter. On velvet paws she slunk away.

A night mist tried to gather: failed – for the air in the gully was too warm – and dissipated into pre-dawn dew. The dampness settled on the children, pressing down their clothes, tracing the outline of their bodies in tiny globules of pearl. They stirred but didn't wake. They were lost in their dreams.

In her sleep the girl moved uneasily. She was in the aeroplane again, and she knew that something was wrong. She and Peter were the only passengers, sandwiched between the crates of vegetables and the frozen carcasses of beef, and she was watching the port engine, waiting for the flames she knew would come. Too soon they were there; the tiny tongues of red licking out of the cowling. In her sleep she twisted and moaned; then mercifully, her mind went blank – nature's safety valve that protects, even in dreams, those who have been shocked beyond endurance – and the next thing she dreamt was that she and Peter were staggering away from the blazing plane, she pulling

8

him frantically because one of his legs was numb and his feet kept sinking into the soft, yielding sand. 'Quick, Peter,' she gasped. 'Quick, before it explodes.' She heard a dull pulsating roar, and looking back saw the figure of the Navigating Officer carrying the pilot and clambering out of the wreckage. In the heat of the explosion he glowed white-hot, disintegrating. Again her mind went numb, but in her sleep she clutched her brother's hand; clutched it and squeezed it so tight that he half-woke and slid awkwardly off her lap.

The nightlights of the fireflies became pale and anaemic. Out of the east crept a permeating greyness; a pearly opaqueness in the sky; the sun-up of another day.

CHAPTER TWO

THE advance guard of sunlight filtered into the gully, turning the night to powdery opaqueness. The warmth of the rays drew this opaqueness up: drew it together into little spirals of mist – random smoke rings from a giant's pipe, that floated lazily above the course of the stream.

As the light gained in intensity, the bush beyond the gully took on new colours: vivid colours: jade and emerald, white and reseda, crimson, scarlet and gold. Here was something very different from the desert of popular imagination; a flowering wilderness of eucalyptus, lantana, brigalow and iron bark. First to take colour were the tops of the eucalyptus: great two-hundred-foot relics of the forests of antiquity, their trunks skeleton white, their oil-laden leaves already twisting edge-on to dodge the shrivelling rays of the sun. The golden light moved lower, gilding the flowered lantana and the straggling brigalow as they intertwined in age-old rivalry; then it came lower still, warming the ridged and furrowed iron bark, the tree that is as hard as studded rhinoceros hide, the tree that never dies (so the Aboriginals say) and is scented more sweetly than orange blossom. At last the golden rays flooded past the outcrop of rock and over the still sleeping children.

The girl lay against the rock, bolstered up by its support. But the boy had moved in the night; he lay sprawled on his back now, arms and legs akimbo. Both slept soundly, unconscious of the growing beauty of the Australian dawn.

On the topmost branch of a gum tree that overhung the gully, there alighted a bird: a large, grey-backed bird, with tufted poll and outsized beak. Its eyes, swivelling separately, searched the gully for food; but instead of the hoped-for frog or snake sunning itself on the rock, it saw the children. The kookaburra was puzzled. The presence of these strange interlopers, it decided, deserved to be announced. It opened wide its beak, and a continuous flow of grating, unmelodious notes shattered the calm of the gully.

The girl leapt to her feet. Her heart pounded. The sweat broke out on the palms of her hands. Terrified, she stared round the sunlit gully.

High above, the kookaburra noted her reactions. Its curiosity was piqued. With another ear-splitting shriek it came swooping down. The girl relaxed. It was only a bird. Its scream was nothing to be frightened of; more to be laughed at really.

She turned to Peter. The kookaburra hadn't disturbed his sleep. Lying beneath the great slab of rock, he looked small and helpless, dwarfed by the immensity of his surroundings. Once again pity and tenderness welled up inside her; brought a pricking feeling to the back of her eyes. How utterly he depended on her now. When he wakes, she thought, he'll be hungry; as hungry as I am. Feeling in the pocket of her frock, she took out the last half-stick of barley sugar; gently she slipped it into her brother's pocket.

Food, she realized, was their immediate problem. Water they could get from the stream, but what could they eat? She knew that people who didn't eat died. She'd read about an explorer once ... it didn't take many days. She looked at the kookaburra. As if sensing her thoughts, he gave a great piercing shriek and went winging down the gully.

But other birds soon took his place: big, black-bodied cockatoos with yellow tails, ripping bark off the eucalyptus in search of grubs; gang-gangs dangling upside-down from the flowers of the lantana; and iridescent painted-finches, splashing merrily in the shallow waters of the creek. The girl watched them. She envied the finches. Already the sun was warm; her dress was dirty and clammy with dew; and the water looked cool and crystal-clear: cool and crystal-clear and tempting. She looked carefully around. Peter was asleep; there was probably no one else within a hundred miles. Impulsively she kicked off her sandals, pulled her frock over her head, stepped out of her panties and ran naked down to the water. The finches darted away. She had the creek to herself.

She found a shallow pool, immediately below a miniature waterfall. Here she slid into the water, watching the ripples lap slowly higher, over her knees, thighs and waist. She was breast deep before her toes touched bottom. Looking down she could see her underwater-self with startling clarity; could even see the bruise on her hip – where she'd crashed

12

against the side of the plane – standing out darkly against the white of her skin. She ducked down till only her floating hair showed on the surface: her long golden hair, the colour of ripening corn, which she started to swirl around and about her like the muleta of a matador. She laughed and splashed and hand-scooped the water over her face, and forgot she was hungry.

Beside the outcrop of rock, her brother stirred. Half-asleep, half-awake, he heard the plash of water. He sat up, yawning and rubbing the sleepiness out of his eyes. For a moment he couldn't think where he was. Then he caught sight of his sister.

'Hi, Mary!' he yelled. 'I'm coming too.'

He scrambled up. Sandals, shorts and shirt were flung aside as he came charging down to the stream. With a reckless belly-flop he arrived beside the girl in a shower of drenching spray.

Mary wasn't pleased. Seizing him under the arm-pits, she plonked him back on the bank.

'Peter, you ass. It's too deep. Look, you're full of water.'

'I'm not. I spat it out. Besides, I can swim.'

He belly-flopped a second time into the pool. But Mary noticed he kept to the shallows now: to the sandy-bottomed shallows where the rivulet widened and the banks flattened out. Watching him, she suddenly became conscious of her nakedness. Quickly she scrambled out of the pool and struggled into her dress.

Peter surveyed her critically.

'You're all wet,' he said. 'You ought to have dried yourself first.'

'Stop chattering, Peter. And get dry yourself.'

She helped him out of the pool, and rubbed him down with his shirt.

'I'm hungry,' he announced cheerfully. 'What can we eat?'

'There's barley sugar in your pocket.'

He pulled out the sticky fragment.

'It's not much.'

He broke it and dutifully offered her half. But she shook her head.

'It's all right,' she said. 'I've had mine.'

She watched him as, cheeks bulging, hands in pockets, he went strolling down by the creek. Thank heavens he didn't seem to be worried: not yet. Whatever happened he must never realize how worried she was; must never lose faith in her ability to look after him.

She watched him exploring their strange surroundings; watched him drop flat on his stomach, and knew he was Davy Crockett, reconnoitring a new frontier. He wriggled along in the sand, cautiously peering across to the farther bank of the stream. Suddenly he leapt to his feet, clutched the seat of his trousers and gave an almighty yell of anguish. Again and again he yelled, as again and again red-hot needles of pain shot through his squirming body.

Mary tumbled and slithered down the rocks; rushed to his aid. For a second she couldn't think what had happened; then she too felt the red-hot needle of pain, and looking down saw their assailants. Ants. Jumping ants. Three-quarters of an inch long, forty per cent jaw and forty per cent powerful grass-hopperish legs. She saw their method of attack at once; saw how they hunched themselves up, then catapulted through the air – often several feet – on to their prey. She half-dragged, half-carried Peter away, at the same time hauling off his trousers.

'It's all right,' she gasped. 'They're only ants. Look. Hanging on to your trousers. Biting away as if you're still inside.'

His wailing stopped; he looked at his discarded shorts. It was true. The ants were still there; their wispy antennae weaving from side to side like the arms of so many punch-drunk boxers; their mandibles were open wide, eager to bite again. But they weren't given the chance. With a shout of rage Peter elbowed his sister aside and started to jump on the shorts; his feet thudded into the denim, pounding and crushing, pulverizing the ants to death. Or so he thought.

Mary stood aside; relieved; half-amused at the violence of his revenge. She had seen the ants sneaking clear of the shorts. But she said nothing. Not until his pounding feet threatened to damage his trousers. Then she reached for his hand.

'O.K., Peter. They're all dead now.'

She helped him on with his shorts.

He started to whimper then; the pain of the bites touching off a host of half-formed fears. Mary's arms went round him. He felt small and shivery and thin; she could feel his heart thudding between his ribs.

'It's all right, Pete,' she whispered. 'I won't let them bite you again.'

His sobs died; but only momentarily. Then they started again.

'What is it, Pete?'

'I don't like this place.'

Now it's coming, she thought. It's coming, and there's nothing I can do about it.

'I don't like it here, Mary. I wanna go home.'

'But we can't go home, Peter. We've got nothing to cross the sea in.'

'Then let's go to Uncle Keith. In Adelaide.'

She was surprised how much he'd remembered. Their plane had been bound for Adelaide.

'All right,' she said slowly. 'I'll take you to Uncle Keith.'

Instantly his sobbing stopped.

'When? Now?'

'Yes,' she said, 'now. We'll start to walk to Adelaide.'

CHAPTER THREE

STURT PLAIN, where the aircraft had crashed, is in the centre of the Northern Territory. It is roughly the size of England and Wales combined; but instead of some 45,000,000 inhabitants, it has roughly 4,500, and instead of some 200,000 roads, it has two, of which one is a fair-weather stock route. Most of the inhabitants are grouped round three or four small towns – Tennant Creek, Hooker Creek, and Daly Waters – which means that the rest of the area is virtually uninhabited. The Plain is fourteen hundred miles from Adelaide and is not a good place to be lost in.

Had they known enough to weigh up their chances, the children would have realized their only hope was to stay beside the wrecked plane; to rely on rescue from the air. But this never occurred to them. Adelaide was somewhere to the south. So southward they started to walk.

The girl worked things out quietly, sensibly – she wasn't the sort to get into a panic. The sun had risen there: on the left of the gully: so that would be east. South, then, must be straight ahead; down-stream. That was lucky. Perhaps they'd be able to follow the creek all the way to the sea; all the way to Adelaide. She knotted the four corners of Peter's handkerchief,

17

dipped it in the water, and draped it over his head –
for already the sun was uncomfortably hot.

'Come on, Peter,' she said, 'let's go.'

She led the way down the gully.

At first the going was easy. Close to the stream,
rocks of granite and quartz provided safe footing; and
the trees, sprouting from every pocket of clay, were
thick enough to give a welcome shade, but not so
thick that they hindered progress. Mary pushed
steadily on.

Soon the gully became wider, flatter, fanning into
an open plain. Another rivulet joined theirs, and
together the two of them went looping away down a
shallow, sand-fringed valley. In the middle of the
valley the undergrowth was thick; luxuriant.
Brambles and underscrub slowed down their progress.
But Mary didn't want to lose sight of the stream. De-
terminedly she forced a way through the tangle of
vegetation, turning every now and then to give her
brother a hand. Ground-vines coiled and snaked and
clutched at their feet; the decaying trunks of fallen
trees perversely blocked their path; but the girl kept
on, sorting out a line of least resistance, holding back
the lower branches to protect Peter from their swing
back.

For two hours the boy followed her manfully; then
he started to lag. Mary noticed at once; she cut across
to the stream and sat down on a shelving slab of
quartz.

'We'll rest now,' she said.

Thankfully he collapsed beside her. She smoothed

18

the hair out of his eyes, plastering it back with its own sweat.

For a long time there was silence; then came the question she had been dreading.

'I'm hungry, Mary. What we going to eat?'

'Oh, Peter! It's not lunch-time yet.'

'When will it be?'

'I'll tell you when.'

But he wasn't satisfied; not satisfied at all.

'When it is time, what we going to eat?'

'I'll find something.'

She didn't tell him that ever since leaving the gully she'd been searching for berries; in vain. But he sensed her anxiety. His mouth started to droop.

'I'm hungry now,' he said.

Quickly she got up.

'All right. Let's look for something to eat.'

To start with – at least for the boy – it was an amusing game: part of their Big Adventure. They looked in the stream for fish; but the fish, such as they were, were asleep: invisible in the sediment-mud. They looked in the trees for birds; but the birds had vanished with the dawn. They looked in the bush for animals; but the animals were all asleep, avoiding the heat of the sun in carefully chosen burrow, log or cave. They looked among the riverside rocks for lizards; but the reptiles heard their clumsy approach, and slid soundlessly into crack or crevice. The bush slept: motionless: silent: apparently deserted. Drugged to immobility by the heat of the midday sun.

The game wasn't amusing for very long.

Eventually their search led them away from the stream, into less luxuriant vegetation; into the open bush. They could see farther here; could see to where, a little way ahead, a ridge of low, slab-sided hills were tilted out of the level plain. The children looked at the hills. They looked friendly; familiar; like the foot-hills of the Alleghenies. The boy reached for his sister's hand.

'Mary!'

'Yes, Peter?'

'Remember when Daddy took us on top of Mount Pleasant. Remember all the lots of sea we could see?'

'Yes, I remember.'

'P'raps we could see the sea from the tops of those mountains.'

It took them half an hour to get to the foot of the hills. They rose in a low escarpment, an outcrop of granite and quartz, jutting abruptly out of the level plain. The stream, moat-like, skirted their feet. There seemed at first to be no way up. Then the girl spotted a dark shadow: a gully, cleaving the escarpment like the cut of an axe.

Except that it faced north rather than south, it might have been the gully where they'd spent the night; it had the same smoothly rising sides, and the same rock-fringed tumbling stream. It took them four hours to climb it.

If the stream hadn't provided them with water, and the sides of the gully with shade, they would never have got to the top.

As it was the sun was setting as they clambered on to the rim of the hills, and saw the country to southward stretching away in front of them, bathed in golden light: a magnificent panorama: a scene of primeval desolation: mile after hundred mile of desert, sand and scrub. And in the far distance, pools of silver; pools of glinting, shimmering light; pools which shivered and wavered and contracted, and seemed to hang a fraction above the horizon.

The boy danced with delight.

'Look, Mary. Look! The sea. The sea. It isn't far to go.'

She caught hold of him and pulled him against her and pressed his face to her breasts.

'Don't look, Peter,' she whispered. 'Don't look again. It isn't fair.'

She knew what the pools of silver were: the salt pans of the great Australian desert. She sat down on the thin tufted grass and started to roll and unroll the hem of her frock.

After a long time she got up, and led the protesting Peter back to the gully. At least there was water there. She told him that tomorrow they'd walk down to the sea. Tomorrow they wouldn't be hungry any more.

CHAPTER FOUR

SUN-UP brought the kookaburras, the gang-gangs and the finches. It brought warmth and colour. And hunger.

The girl woke early. She lay on her back, thinking. Outwardly she was calm; but inwardly she was damming back a gathering flood of fear. Always she had protected Peter, had smoothed things out and made them easy for him – molly-coddled him like an anxious hen her father had once said. But how could she protect him now? She knew that soon he'd be awake; awake and demanding to start off for the 'sea'. It would be too cruel to tell him the sea wasn't there. She'd have to think of something else: have to tell him one of those special sort of lies that Mummy said God didn't mind. Her forehead puckered in concentrated thought.

Too soon Peter was awake.

*

They spent the morning searching for food. It would be foolish, Mary said, to start walking seaward without having something to eat; without first collecting a stock of food for their journey. The sea might be farther off than it looked.

They searched mainly for fruit, but for a long time found nothing. They examined the tawny leopardtrees, the sapless mellowbane, the humble-bushes with their frightened collapsing leaves, and the blood-woods with their overflowing crimson sap. They skirted the kurrajungs and the bottlebrushes and the eucalyptus; then they came to a group of trees of another, rarer kind: graceful, symmetrical trees, covered with thick silver foliage and – miracle of miracles – with multicoloured globules of fruit.

Peter gave a whoop of delight, and rushed headlong at the longed-for food. For a second Mary hung back, thinking of poison; then she too was leaping and snatching at the balls of fruit. It was a chance they'd have to take.

The fruit – called *quondong* by the Aboriginals – was about the size of ping-pong balls, and ranged in colour from greengage-green to plum-red. The redder fruit, they quickly found, were the riper. To the starving children they were ambrosia; sweet and juicy, thirst-quenching and nourishing. They ate, and ate, and ate.

For a long time they sat in the shade of the *quon-dong* trees, the trees that had saved their lives. They were too happy to talk.

After a while Mary got up and began to pick more of the fruit: their cache for the trek to the sea. She hummed contentedly as she collected the *quondong*, storing them first in Peter's handkerchief then in the folds of her dress. Soon Peter also got up; he wandered across to one of the trees and started lazily to gather the fruit. Working their way from tree to tree, the children drifted slowly apart.

Though the edge had gone from his hunger, Peter wasn't altogether at ease. He kept looking nervously at the surrounding bush. He had a strange sort of feeling: a feeling of being watched. Several times he looked up quickly, certain there was someone there; but the bush slept on in the heat of the sun: silent, motionless, apparently deserted. Unconvinced, he sidled back to his sister.

'Mary!' he whispered. 'I think there's someone here!'

'Someone here! Where?'

Disbelieving she swung round. The *quondong* fell to the grass. Only by snapping her teeth together did she stifle a scream of fear. For there, less than four feet away, so close that she could have stretched out an arm and touched him, was a boy. And he was ebony black and quite naked.

CHAPTER FIVE

THE girl's first impulse was to grab Peter and run; but as her eyes swept over the stranger, her fear died slowly away. The boy was young – certainly no older than she was; he was unarmed, and his attitude was more inquisitive than threatening: more puzzled than hostile.

He wasn't the least bit like an African Negro. His skin was certainly black, but beneath it was a curious hint of undersurface bronze, and it was fine-grained: glossy, satiny, almost silk-like. His hair wasn't crinkly but nearly straight; and his eyes were blue-black: big, soft and inquiring. In his hand was a baby rock wallaby, its eyes, unclosed in death, staring vacantly above a tiny pointed snout.

All this Mary noted and accepted. The thing that she couldn't accept, the thing that seemed to her shockingly and indecently wrong, was the fact that the boy was naked.

The three children stood looking at each other in the middle of the Australian desert. Motionless as the outcrops of granite they stared, and stared, and stared. Between them the distance was less than the spread of an outstretched arm, but more than a hundred thousand years.

Brother and sister were products of the highest

strata of humanity's evolution. In them the primitive had long ago been swept aside, been submerged by mechanization, been swamped by scientific development, been nullified by the standardized pattern of the white man's way of life. They had climbed a long way up the ladder of progress; they had climbed so far, in fact, that they had forgotten how their climb had started. Coddled in babyhood, psycho-analysed in childhood, nourished on predigested patent foods, provided with continuous push-button entertainment, the basic realities of life were something they'd never had to face.

It was very different with the Aboriginal. He knew what reality was. He led a way of life that was already old when Tut-ankh-amen started to build his tomb; a way of life that had been tried and proved before the white man's continents were even lifted out of the sea. Among the secret water-holes of the Australian desert his people had lived and died, unchanged and unchanging, for twenty thousand years. Their lives were unbelievably simple. They had no homes, no crops, no clothes, no possessions. The few things they had, they shared: food and wives; children and laughter; tears and hunger and thirst. They walked from one water-hole to the next; they exhausted one supply of food, then moved on to another. Their lives were utterly uncomplicated because they were devoted to one purpose, dedicated in their entirety to the waging of one battle: the battle with death. Death was their ever-present enemy. He sought them out from every dried-up salt pan, from the flames of every bush fire. He was never far away. Keeping him at bay was the Aboriginals' full-time job: the job they'd been doing for twenty thousand years: the job they were good at.

The desert sun streamed down. The children stared and stared.

Mary had decided not to move. To move would be a sign of weakness. She remembered being told about the man who'd come face to face with a lion, and had stared it out, had caused it to slink discomfited away. That was what she'd do to the black boy; she'd stare at him until he felt the shame of his nakedness and slunk away. She thrust out her chin, and glared.

Peter had decided to take his cue from his sister. Clutching her hand he stood waiting: waiting for something to happen.

The Aboriginal was in no hurry. Time had little value to him. His next meal – the rock wallaby – was assured. Water was near. Tomorrow was also a day. For the moment he was content to examine these strange creatures at his leisure. Their clumsy, lumbering movements intrigued him; their lack of weapons indicated their harmlessness. His eyes moved slowly, methodically from one to another: examining them from head to foot. They were the first white people a member of his tribe had ever seen.

Mary, beginning to resent this scrutiny, intensified her glare. But the bush boy seemed in no way perturbed; his appraisal went methodically on.

After a while Peter started to fidget. The delay was fraying his nerves. He wished someone would do something: wished something would happen. Then, quite involuntarily, he himself started a new train of events. His head began to waggle; his nose tilted skywards; he spluttered and choked; he tried to hold his breath; but all in vain. It had to come. He sneezed.

It was a mighty sneeze for such a little fellow: the release of a series of concatenated explosions, all the more violent for having been dammed back.

To his sister the sneeze was a calamity. She had just intensified her stare to the point – she felt sure – of irresistibility, when the spell was shattered. The bush boy's attention shifted from her to Peter.

Frustration warped her sense of justice. She condemned her brother out of court; was turning on him angrily, when a second sneeze, even mightier than the first, shattered the silence of the bush.

Mary raised her eyes to heaven: invoking the gods as witnesses to her despair. But the vehemence of the second sneeze was still tumbling leaves from the humble-bushes, when a new sound made her whirl around. A gust of laughter: melodious laughter; low at first, then becoming louder: unrestrained: disproportionate: uncontrolled.

She looked at the bush boy in amazement. He was doubled up with belly-shaking spasms of mirth.

Peter's incongruous, out-of-proportion sneeze had touched off one of his peoples' most highly developed traits: a sense of the ridiculous; a sense so keenly felt as to be almost beyond control. The bush boy laughed with complete abandon. He flung himself to the ground. He rolled head-over-heels in unrestrained delight.

His mirth was infectious. It woke in Peter an instant response: a like appreciation of the ludicrous. The guilt that the little boy had started to feel, melted away. At first apologetically, then whole-heartedly, he too started to laugh.

The barrier of twenty thousand years vanished in the twinkling of an eye.

The boys' laughter echoed back from the granite rocks. They started to strike comic postures, each striving to outdo the other in their grotesque abandon.

Mary watched them. She would have dearly loved to join in. A year ago – in her tom-boy days – she would have. But not now. She was too sensible: too grown-up. Yet not grown-up enough to be free of an instinctive longing to share in the fun: to throw convention to the winds and join the capering jamboree. This longing she repressed. She stood aloof: disapproving. At last she went up to Peter and took his hand.

'That's enough, Peter,' she said.

The skylarking subsided. For a moment there was silence, then the bush boy spoke.

'*Worumgala?*' (Where do you come from?) His voice was lilting as his laughter.

Mary and Peter looked at each other blankly.

The bush boy tried again.

'*Worum mwa?*' (Where are you going?)

It was Peter, not Mary, who floundered into the field of conversation.

'We dun'no what you're talking about, darkie. But we're lost, see. We want to go to Adelaide. That's where Uncle Keith lives. Which way do we go?'

The black boy grinned. To him the little one's voice was comic as his appearance: half-gabble, half-chirp; and shrill, like a baby magpie's. Peter grinned back, eager for another orgy of laughter. But the bush boy wanted to be serious now. He stepped noiselessly up to Peter, brushed his fingers over the boy's face, then looked at them expectantly; but to his surprise the whiteness hadn't come off. He ran his fingers through Peter's hair. Again he was surprised; no powdered clay, nor red-ochre paste. He turned his attention to the white boy's clothes.

Peter was by no means perturbed. On the contrary he felt flattered; proud. He realized that the bush boy had never seen anything like him before. He held himself very straight, swelled out his chest, and turned slowly round and round.

The bush boy's dark tapering fingers plucked gently at his shirt, following the line of the seams, testing the strength of the criss-cross weave, exploring the mystery of the buttonholes. Then his attention passed from shirt to shorts. Peter became suddenly loquacious.

'Those are shorts, darkie. Short pants. You oughta have 'em too. To cover your bottom up. Haven't you any shops round here?'

The bush boy refused to be diverted. He had found the broad band of elastic that kept the shorts in place. While he fingered it, the white boy prattled on.

30

'That's elastic that is; keeps your shorts in place. It stretches. Look!'

He stuck his thumbs into the waist-band, pulled the elastic away from his hips, then let it fly back. The resounding smack made the bush boy jump. Thoroughly pleased with himself Peter repeated the performance, this time adding a touch of pantomime, staggering backward as if he'd been struck. The black boy saw the joke. He grinned, but this time he kept his laughter under control; for his examination was a serious business. He ended up with a detailed inspection of Peter's sandals.

Then he turned to Mary.

It was the moment the girl had been dreading.

Yet she didn't draw back. She wanted to; God alone knew how she wanted to. Her nerves were strung taut. The idea of being manhandled by a naked black boy appalled her: struck at the root of one of the basic principles of her civilized code. It was terrifying; revolting; obscene. Back in Charleston it would have got the darkie lynched. Yet she didn't move; not even when the dark fingers ran like spiders up and down her body.

She stayed motionless because, deep-down, she knew she had nothing to fear. The things that she'd been told way back in Charleston were somehow not applicable any more. The values she'd been taught to cherish became suddenly meaningless. A little guilty, a little resentful, and more than a little bewildered, she waited passively for whatever might happen next.

The bush boy's inspection didn't take long. The

larger of these strange creatures, he saw at once, was much the same as the smaller – except that the queer things draped around it were, if possible, even more ludicrous. Almost perfunctorily his fingers ran over Mary's face, frock and sandals; then he stepped back: satisfied. There was nothing more he wanted to know.

Turning to where the dead rock wallaby lay in the sand, he picked it up. Odd ants had found it: were nosing through its fur. The boy brushed them off. Then he walked quietly away; away down the valley; soon he was out of sight.

*

The children couldn't believe it; couldn't believe that he'd really left them. It was all so sudden: so utterly unexpected.

Peter was first to grasp what had happened.

'Mary!' his voice was frightened. 'He's gone!'

The girl said nothing. She was torn by conflicting emotions. Relief that the naked black boy had disappeared, and regret that she hadn't asked him for help; fear that nobody could help them anyhow, and a sneaking feeling that perhaps if anyone could it had been the black boy. A couple of days ago she'd have known what to do; known what was best; known how to act. But she didn't know now. Uncertain, she hid her face in her hands.

It was Peter who made the decision. In the bush boy's laughter he'd found something he liked: a lifeline he didn't intend to lose.

'Hey, Mary!' he gasped. 'Come on. After him!'

He went crashing into the bush. Slowly, doubtfully, his sister followed.

'Hey darkie!' Peter's reedy treble echoed down the valley. 'We wanna come too. Wait for us!'

'Hey, darkie!' the rocks re-echoed. 'Wait for us. Wait for us. Wait for us.'

CHAPTER SIX

THE bush boy turned. He knew what the call meant: the strangers were coming after him, were following him down the valley; already he could hear them crashing and lumbering through the scrub.

He waited; relaxed both physically and mentally: one hand passed behind his back and closed round the opposite elbow; one foot, ostrich-like, resting on the calf of the opposite leg. He wasn't frightened, for he knew instinctively that the strangers were harmless as a pair of tail-less kangaroos; but he *was* mildly surprised, for he had thought them both, especially the larger, impatient, eager to be on their way. As the children came racing towards him, he dropped his foot to the ground; became suddenly all attention; full of curiosity to know what they wanted to say and how they were going to say it.

Peter launched into a breathless appeal.

'Hey, don't leave us, darkie! We're lost. We want food, an' drink. And we wanna know how we get to Adelaide.'

Mary looked at the bush boy, and saw in his eyes a gleam of amusement. It angered her, for she knew the cause; Peter's high-pitched, corncrakey voice. All the tenets of progressive society and racial superiority combined inside her to form a deep-rooted core of resentment. It was wrong, cruelly wrong, that she and her brother should be forced to run for help to a Negro; and a naked Negro at that. She clutched Peter's hand, half drawing him away.

But Peter was obsessed by none of his sister's scruples. To him their problem was simple, uncomplicated: they wanted help, and here was someone who could, his instinct told him, provide it. The fact that his appeal had failed to register first time nonplussed him for a moment. But he wasn't put off; he stuck to his guns. Breath and composure regained, he now spoke slowly, in a lower, less excited key.

'Look, darkie, we're lost. We want water. You sabby water? War-tur. War-tur.'

He cupped his hands together, drew them up to his lips, and went through the motions of swallowing.

The bush boy nodded.

'*Arkooloola.*"

His eyes were serious now. Understanding. Sympathetic. He knew what it meant to be thirsty.

'*Arkooloola.*"

He said the word again. Softly, musically, like the rippling of water over rock. He pursed up his lips and moved them as though he, too, were drinking.

Peter hopped delightedly from foot to foot.

'That's it, darkie. You've got it. *Arkooloolya.* That's the stuff we want. And food too. You sabby food? Foo-ood. Foo-ood.'

He went through the motions of cutting with knife and fork, then started to champ his jaws.

The cutting meant nothing to the bush boy; but the jaw champing did. Again his eyes were sympathetic.

'*Yeemara.*'

His teeth, in unison with Peter's, clicked in understanding.

The white boy was jubilant.

'You've got it, darkie. Got it first time. *Yeemara* an' *Arkooloolya*. That's the stuff we want. Now where do we get 'em?'

The bush boy turned, moved away at right angles, into the scrub. He paused, glanced over his shoulder, then moved away again.

'*Kurura*,' he said.

There was no mistaking his meaning.

'Come on, Mary,' the boy hissed excitedly. '*Kurura*, that means "follow me".'

He trotted eagerly after the bush boy.

Slowly, reluctantly, the girl followed.

After a while they came to a forest of heartleaves. Beneath the thick, closely-woven foliage the shade was deep: a striking contrast to the glare of the bush. Beneath the close-packed trees the white children moved uncertainly, stumblingly: their sun-narrowed pupils slow to adjust themselves to the sudden darkness. But the bush boy, his eyes refocussing almost at once, pushed rapidly on. The others, stumbling and tripping over ground roots, were hard put to keep up with him.

It was cool beneath the heartleaves; cool and quiet and motionless as a sylvan stage set. Hour after hour the bush boy led on, gliding like a bar of well-oiled shadow among the giant trees. He moved without apparent effort, yet quickly enough for Peter to be forced to jog-trot. Soon the small boy was panting. In spite of the shade, sweat plastered back his hair; trickled round his eyes and into his mouth. He started to lag behind. Seeing him in trouble, Mary also dropped back; and Peter reached for her hand.

The girl was pleased: gratified that in his difficulties he'd turned to her. Subconscious twinges of jealousy had been tormenting her. She had been hurt, deeply hurt, at his so quickly transferring his sense of reliance from her to an uncivilized and naked black. But now things were returning to normal; now he was coming back to the sisterly fold.

'All right, Peter,' she whispered, 'we won't leave you behind.'

She knew that he must – like her – be suffering cruelly from thirst, hunger, and physical exhaustion: knew that his mouth, like hers, must feel as if it were crammed with red-hot cotton wool. But there was nothing they could do about it: or would it, she wondered, help if they acted like dogs – lolled out their tongues and panted?

Ahead of them the heartleaves ended abruptly. One moment they were groping forward in deep shade, the next they were looking out across an expanse of glaring sand: mile after shimmering mile of ridge and dune, salt-pan and iron-rock: the Sturt Desert: heat-hazed, sun-drenched, waterless.

'*Kurura*,' the bush boy said.

He started to walk into the desert.

Mary held back. She didn't exactly mistrust the bush boy, didn't doubt that if he wished he could – eventually – lead them to food and water. But how far away would the food and water be? Too far, most likely, for them ever to reach it. She sank to her knees in the shade of the last of the heartleaves. Peter collapsed beside her; the sweat from his hair ran damply into the lap of her dress.

The bush boy came back. He spoke softly, urgently, the pitch of his words rising and falling like the murmur of wavelets on a sandy shore. The words themselves were meaningless; but his gestures spoke plainly enough. If they stayed where they were they would die: the bush boy fell to the sand, his fingers scrabbling the dry earth; soon the evil spirits would come to molest their bodies; the bush boy's eyes rolled in terror. But if they followed him he would take them to water; the bush boy swallowed and gulped. They hadn't far to go: only as far as the hill-that-had-fallen-out-of-the-moon; his finger pointed to a strange outcrop of rock that rose like a gargantuan cairn out of the desert, a cairn the base of which was circled by a dark, never-moving shadow.

It looked very far away.

The girl wiped the sweat out of her eyes. In the shade of the heartleaves it was mercifully cool; far cooler than it would be in the desert. It would be so much easier, she thought, to give the struggle up, simply to stay where they were. She looked at the cairn critically. How could the bush boy know there was water there? Whoever heard of finding water on top of a pile of rock in the middle of a desert?

'Arkooloola,' the bush boy insisted. He said it again and again, pointing to the base of the cairn.

The girl looked more closely, shading her eyes against the glare of the sun. She noticed that there was something strange about the shadow at the foot of the cairn. As far as she could see, it went all the way round. It couldn't, then, be ordinary shadow, caused by the sun. What else, she wondered, could create such a circle of shade? The answer came suddenly, in a flood of wonder and disbelief. It must be vegetation. Trees and bushes: thick, luxuriant, verdant, and lush. And such vegetation, she knew, could only spring from continually-watered roots. She struggled to her feet.

It seemed a long way to the hill-that-had-fallen-out-of-the-moon. By the time they got there the sun was setting.

They came to the humble-bushes first, the twitching, quivering leaves tumbling to the sand as they approached. Then came the straw-like mellowbane, and growing amongst them a grass of a very different kind: sturdy reed-thick grass, each blade tipped with a black, bean-shaped nodule: rustling death-rattle, astir in the sunset wind. The bush boy snapped off one of the reeds. He drove it into the sand. Its head, when he pulled it out, was damp. He smiled encouragement.

'Arkooloola,' he said, and hurried on.

The base of the cairn rose steeply, strata upon strata of terraced iron-rock rising sheer from the desert floor; and the bottom belt of strata was moss-coated and glistening damp, with lacy maidenhair and filigree spider-fern trailing from every crevice. The children stumbled on, brushing aside the umbrella ferns, spurred forward now by the plash of water and by a sudden freshness in the air.

Peter had been lagging behind – for the last mile Mary had been half-carrying, half-dragging him. But now, like an iron filing drawn to a magnet, he broke loose and went scurrying ahead. He disappeared into the shade of the umbrella ferns, and a second later Mary heard his hoarse, excited shout.

'It's water, Mary! Water.'

'Arkooloola,' the bush boy grinned.

Together black boy and white girl pushed through the tangle of fern until they came to a tiny pear-shaped basin carved out of solid rock by the ceaseless drip of water. Beside the basin Peter was flat on his face, his head, almost up to his ears, dunked in the clear translucent pool. In a second Mary was flat out beside him. Both children drank, and drank, and drank.

The water was luke-warm; for though the sun was no longer shining on it directly, the all-pervading heat had found it out: had warmed it almost to the temperature of blood. As the girl drank she saw, out of the corner of her eye, the bush boy settle down beside her. She noticed that he didn't drink from the surface, but reached down, with his fingers outspread, to scoop water from the bottom of the pool. Quick to learn, she too reached down to the rocky bottom. At once the warm surface water was replaced by a current of surprising coolness: a delicious eddy from depths that the rays of the sun had never plumbed. Nectar, with a coolness doubly stimulating: doubly good.

The bush boy drank only a little. Soon he got to his feet, climbed a short way up the cairn, and settled himself on a ledge of rock. Warm in the rays of the setting sun, he watched the strangers with growing curiosity. Not only, he decided, were they freakish in appearance and clumsy in movement, they were also amazingly helpless: untaught; unskilled, utterly incapable of fending for themselves: perhaps the last survivors of some peculiarly backward tribe. Unless he looked after them, they would die. That was certain. He looked at the children critically; but there was in his appraisal no suggestion of scorn. It was his people's way to accept individuals as they were: to help, not to criticize, the sick, the blind, and the maimed.

He noticed that the smaller of the pair had finished drinking now, and was climbing awkwardly towards him. He leant down, and hauled him on to the ledge of rock.

The water had revived a good deal of Peter's vitality. He was coming now to do something that his sister couldn't bring herself to do: to beg for food. His eyes were on the baby wallaby, still held in the

41

bush boy's hand. He reached out and touched it; tentatively; questioningly.

'Eat?' he said. '*Yeemara?*'

*

The sun was setting as the boys clambered down from the rock. Twilight, in the Northern Territory, is short. In half an hour it would be quite dark.

The bush boy moved quickly. Skirting the outcrop of rock, he came to a place where a chain of billabongs went looping into the desert: baby poollets, fed from the main pool's overflowing breast. Beside the last of the billabongs was an area of soft sandstone rock: flat, featureless, devoid of vegetation. Here, the bush boy decided, was the site for their fire. He started to clear the area of leaves, twigs, and grass; everything inflammable he swept aside; so that the evil spirits of the bush fire should have nothing to feed on.

Peter watched him. Inquisitive. Imitative. Soon he too started to brush away the leaves and pluck out the blades of grass. And as he worked he fired off questions; his chirpy falsetto echoing shrilly among the rocks.

'What you reckonin' to do, darkie? What you sweepin' the rock like it was a carpet for?'

The bush boy grinned; he'd guessed what the small one wanted to know. On the palm of his hand he placed a dried leaf and a fragment of resin-soaked yacca-yacca; then he blew on them gently, carefully, as though he were coaxing a reluctant flame.

'*Larana,*' he said.

'I get it!' Peter was jubilant. 'Fire. You're gonna light a fire.'

'*Larana*,' the bush boy insisted.

'O.K., darkie. *Larana* then. You're gonna light a *Larana*. I'll help.'

He buckled to; pouncing on bits of debris like a hungry chicken pecking at scattered corn. The bush boy clicked his teeth in approval.

From the edge of the pool Mary watched them. Again she felt a stab of jealousy, mingled this time with envy. She tried to fight it: told herself it was wrong to feel this way. But the jealousy wouldn't altogether die. She sensed the magnetic call of boy to boy: felt left-out, alone. If only she too had been a boy! She lay quietly, face-downward on the rocks, chin in hands, watching.

Peter followed the bush boy slavishly, copying his every move. Together, with sharp flints, they scooped a hollow out of the sandstone: about three feet square and nine inches deep. Then they started to forage for wood. They found it in plenty along the fringe of the desert. Yacca-yaccas: their tall, eight-foot poles, spear-straight, rising out of the middle of every tuffet of grass. The bush boy wrenched out the older poles: those that were dry, brittle with the saplessness of age. Then, amongst the roots, he fossicked for resin; the exuded sap that had overflowed from and run down the yacca-yaccas' stems in the days of their prime. This resin was dry and wax-like: easily combustible; nature's ready-made firelighter.

Following the bush boy's example, Peter snapped

off the smaller poles, and hunted assiduously for resin.

Then came the snapping of the wood into burnable fragments, and the grinding of the resin into a gritty powder; then the collecting of stones (not the moisture-impregnated rock from around the billa-bongs – which was liable to explode when heated – but the flat, flinty, saucer-shaped stones of the desert). And at last the preparations were finished: the fire was ready to be lit.

The bush boy selected a large, smooth-surfaced chip, cut a groove along its centre, then placed it in the hollow in the sandstone. Next he took a slender stem of yacca, and settled the end of it into the groove of the chip. The chip was then covered with wood splinters and sprinkled with powdered resin. Placing an open palm on either side of the yacca stem, the bush boy rubbed his hands together. Slowly at first, then faster and faster, the stem revolved in the groove, creating first friction then heat.

As the sun sank under the rim of the desert, a lazy spiral of wood-smoke rose into the evening air.

The bush boy's hands twisted faster. This was the skill that raised him above the level of the beasts. Bird can call to bird, and animal to animal; mother dingoes can sacrifice themselves for their young; termites can live in highly-organized communal towns. But they can't make fire. Man alone can harness the elements.

A blood-red glow suffused the resin. The glow

spread; brightened; burst into flame. The boys piled on the sticks of yacca. The fire was made.

The bush boy collected the wallaby; held it by tail-tip over the flames; scorched it down to the bare skin. Then he laid it in the hollow. After a while he picked up a stick and started to lever the fire-heated stones on top of the carcass. Then he banked up the hollow with earth and ash. The rock wallaby baked gently.

*

An hour later they were eating it, watched by a single dingo and a thin crescent moon. It skinned easily; the flesh was succulent and tender; and there was enough for all.

Before they settled down to sleep the bush boy scattered the fire; stamped out every spark, smoothed out every heap of ash. Then, like a blackstone sentinel, he stood for a while beside the loop of the billabongs, gazing into the desert, interpreting sounds that the children couldn't even hear. Eventually, satisfied that all was well, he lay down close to the others on the slab of sandstone rock.

A veil of cumulus drifted over the moon.

After a while the dingo crept out of the bush and on to the ledge of sandstone; warily he nosed through the ashes for bones; but he found none. A pair of flying foxes flip-flapped down to the billabong. Little folds of mist moved softly round the hill-that-had-fallen-out-of-the-moon. And the children slept.

CHAPTER SEVEN

T HE girl woke early: in the whiteness and still-
ness of the false dawn: in the hour before sunrise
when the light is very clear and the earth peculiarly still. She lay on her back, watching the stars
die and the sky pale. Was heaven there, she wondered;
somewhere beyond the stars and sky? If it hadn't been
for the bush boy she'd probably know by now. She
rolled on to her side and looked at the naked
Aboriginal, then looked quickly away. If only she,
too, had been a boy!

She tried to think calmly, logically. One thing she
was certain of: the bush boy had saved their lives.
He was used to living in the desert. That was obvious.
So long as they stayed with him they'd probably
keep alive. But they'd still be lost. Could they, she
wondered, persuade him to take them all the way to
Adelaide? But perhaps he didn't know where Adelaide
was ... She wondered what he was doing, wandering
the desert alone, far from family or tribe. It was all
very puzzling.

A few weeks ago she'd have known what to do;
known what was best. But here in the desert most of
the old rules and the old values seemed strangely
meaningless. Uncertain, unsure, she fell back on a

woman's oldest line-of-action: passivity. She'd simply wait and see.

The decision brought immediate relief. Now she'd relinquished her leadership and all its implied responsibility, much of her keyed-up tension ebbed away. Rolling on to her back she closed her eyes and fell almost at once into a deep refreshing sleep.

She woke, a couple of hours later, to the sound of laughter and splashing water. Sitting up, she saw her brother and the black boy bathing in the billabong. They were ducking each other beneath a miniature waterfall that cascaded down from the rock.

'Come on, Mary,' her brother shouted. 'In with us.'

'Come on, Mary,' the rocks re-echoed. 'In with us. In with us.'

She waved cheerfully.

'Later,' she shouted. 'When it's warmer.'

Peter opened his mouth to remonstrate; but his mouth filled suddenly with water; the bush boy had ducked him again. Peter flailed his arms. Like a miniature waterspout he rushed his assailant. The bush boy feigned defeat; in mock terror he fled across the billabong; splashing through the shallows, still pursued by Peter, he clambered on to the farther bank. There he paused. Even in play, part of his attention had been subconsciously focused on the ever-present problem of survival, the never satisfied search for food. Now, close to the billabong, he started to probe at a cluster of bulb-shaped protuberances in the sand. With his long prehensile toes he scratched away the top soil, uncovering a soft, brown-skinned ball, about the size of a coconut.

'Worwora!' his voice was excited.

Peter came scrambling out of the water. Doubtfully, he looked at the ball; hopefully, he touched it.

'Yeemara?' he asked.

The bush boy nodded, and together they started to unearth the strange coconut ball. It was one of nature's paradoxes: a plant growing upside-down: a leaf and flower-bearing liana whose foliage grew entirely under the ground. Close to the surface was the tuber-like yam; spread out around and beneath it were its flowers and leaves, drawing from the soil that sustenance which the air of the desert denied. It was a plant as rare as it was strange, and as tasty as it looked unpalatable.

The bush boy broke off the yam; then, following another skein of underground foliage, he tracked down a second. Fascinated, Peter watched. He got the idea quickly. Soon he too had sought out and pulled up a third worwora. The bush boy grinned in appreciation. The little one was quick to learn. Following the lines of underground foliage, the two boys worked gradually away from the billabong. Soon, side by side, they disappeared into the desert.

When they were out of sight Mary came down to the chain of pools. Soon she too was laughing and splashing under the waterfall. But she listened carefully for sound of the boys' return. As soon as she heard their voices, she scrambled out of the water, and quickly pulled on her dress.

The boys' arms were full: full of *worworas*. They were carrying at least a dozen each; and they were, Mary suddenly noticed, both of them quite naked. She picked up her brother's shorts from beside the edge of the billabong.

'Peter,' she said, 'come here.'

He came reluctantly across.

'Gee! I don't need no clothes, Mary. It's too hot.'

'Put them on,' she said.

He recognized her strict governess's voice.

A week ago he wouldn't have dreamt of arguing. But somehow he felt different here in the desert. He looked at his sister defiantly, weighing the odds of revolt.

'O.K.,' he said at last. 'I'll wear the shorts. But nothing else.'

A week ago the girl wouldn't have stood for conditions. But somehow, for her too, things were different now. She accepted the compromise without complaint.

*

They cooked the yam-like plants in the reheated ash of last night's hearth. They tasted good: sweet and pulpy: a cross between potato, artichoke, and parsnip.

During the meal Mary watched the black boy. They owed him their lives. His behaviour was impeccable. He was healthy and scrupulously clean. All this she admitted. Yet his nakedness still appalled her. She felt guilty every time she looked at him. If only he, like Peter, would wear a pair of shorts! She told herself it wasn't his fault that he was naked: told herself that he must be one of those unfortunate people one prayed for in church – 'the people who knew not Thy word': the people the missionaries still hadn't caught. Missionaries, she knew, were people who put black boys into trousers. Her father had said so – 'trousers for the boys,' he'd said, 'and shimmy-shirts for the girls.' But the missionaries, alas, evidently hadn't got round to Australia yet. Perhaps that's why it was called the lost continent. Suddenly an idea came to her. A flash of inspiration. She'd be the first Australian missionary.

Missionaries, she knew, were people who made sacrifices for others. While the boys were scattering ash from the fire, she moved to the far side of the cairn, hitched up her dress, and slipped out of her panties.

Then she walked across to the bush boy, and touched him on the shoulder.

She felt compassionate: charitable: virtuous. Like a dignitary bestowing some supremely precious gift, she handed her panties to the naked Aboriginal.

He took them shyly: wonderingly: not knowing what they were for. He put the *worwora* down, and examined the gift more closely. His fingers explored the elastic top. Its flick-back was something he didn't understand. (Bark thread and liana vine didn't behave like this.) He stretched the elastic taut; tested it; experimented with it, was trying to unravel it when Peter came to his aid.

'Hey, don't undo 'em, darkie! Put 'em on. One foot in here, one foot in there. Then pull 'em up.'

The words were meaningless to the bush boy, but the small one's miming was clear enough. He was cautious at first: suspicious of letting himself be hobbled. Yet his instinct told him that the strangers meant him no harm; that their soft, bark-like offering was a gift, a token of gratitude. It would be impolite to refuse. Helped by Peter, he climbed carefully into the panties.

Mary sighed with relief. Decency had been restored. Her missionary zeal had been blessed with its just reward.

But Peter looked at the bush boy critically. There was something wrong: something incongruous. He couldn't spot the trouble at first. Then, quite suddenly, he saw it: the lace-edge to the panties. He tried his hardest not to laugh – his sister, he knew, wouldn't approve of his laughing. He clapped a hand to his mouth; but it was no good; it had to come. Like a baby kookaburra he suddenly exploded into a shrill and unmelodious cackle. Then, giving way to uninhibited delight, he started to caper round and round the bush boy. His finger shot out.

'Look! Look! He's got lacy panties on. Sissy girl! Sissy girl! Sissy girl!'

Faster and faster he whirled his mocking fandango.

Mary was horrified. But for the bush boy, Peter's antics supplied the half-expected cue. He knew for certain now why the strange gift had been made, knew what it signified: the prelude to a jamboree, the dressing-up that heralded the start of a ritual dance. The little one had started the dancing; now it was up to him to keep it going. He did so with wholehearted zest.

The joyful caperings of Peter were nothing compared to the contortions the bush boy now went into. He leapt and bounded around the billabong with the abandon of a dervish run amok. It was a symbolic combat he danced; a combat in which he was both victor and vanquished; a combat between life and death. He had no emu feathers in his hair, no moistened ochre streaking his face and chest; but he snatched up a stem of yacca-yacca for spear and a splinter of ironbark for club, and jabbing, dodging, feinting and parrying he fought his pantomime self to exhaustion. It was the only dance he knew: the war dance; the natural and inevitable sequel to dressing-up.

Brother and sister watched his act, first in amazement, then in unrestrained delight.

'Kup, kup, yurr-rr-rr-a! Kup, kup, kurr-rr-rra!'

The bush boy's war cry started like the yap of an attacking dingo and ended in the bush-dog's throat-shaking growl. He became utterly lost in his battle; the pantomime became reality. First he was the triumphant attacker; in and out the yacca-yacca darted like the jab of a fish-barbed spear; round and about the ironbark flailed, battering, parrying, crushing. Then he transferred himself to the receiving end. He clutched at his chest, wrenching out the imagined fish-barbs; he smote his forehead, smashing himself to the sand; dazedly he staggered up. But with an ear-splitting howl of victory his assailant was on him. The spear stabbed through his heart. With a choking cry the defeated warrior toppled from the crest of a sand-dune; in a grotesque, stiff-limbed somersault, he slid to the desert floor. Then he lay still. The battle was over; but the victory parade was still to come.

Like a phoenix rising, the victor sprang from the vanquished's body. His fists he clenched and knotted above his head – like a boxer self-acknowledging his prowess. His feet he pulled proudly up in a high-kicking march of victory – an ebullient, primitive goose-step. And after every so many paces he leapt high into the air and brought both heels up from behind, to strike himself on the buttocks with a resounding, flesh-tingling slap. At first the tempo of the victory dance was slow and measured: stylized. But gradually it quickened. The goose-stepping became higher, faster; the leaping more frenzied, more abandoned. The bush boy's body glistened with sweat. His breathing quickened. His nostrils dilated. His eyes rolled. Yet still the dance went on: ever faster, ever wilder. He was swaying now to a drumbeat that couldn't be heard, caught up in a ritual that couldn't be broken. On and on and on; though his muscles were aching, his lungs bursting, his heart pounding, and his mind empty as the cloudless sky. Then suddenly the climax: somersault after somersault, victory-roll after victory-roll, till he was standing, stock still and in sudden silence, face to face with the children.

And once again he was naked; for at the moment of climax the elastic of the panties had snapped, and the gift – symbol of civilization – lay under his feet, trampled into the desert sand.

White girl and black boy, a couple of yards apart, stood staring one at another.

The girl's eyes grew wider and wider.

The bush boy's eyes widened too. He realized, quite suddenly, that the larger of the strangers wasn't a male: she was a lubra, a budding gin.

He took a half-pace forward. Then he drew back. Appalled. For into the girl's eyes there came a terror such as he'd seen only a couple of times before: a terror that could for him have only one meaning, one tragic and inevitable cause. He began to tremble then, in great, uncontrolled, nerve-jerking spasms. For, to him, the girl's terror could only mean one thing: that she had seen in his eyes an image: the image of the Spirit of Death.

CHAPTER EIGHT

To the bush boy everything had its appointed time. There was a time to be weaned, a time to be carried in arms: a time to walk with the tribe, a time to walk alone: a time for the proving-of-manhood, a time for the taking of gins. A time for hunting, and a time to die. These times were pre-ordained. They never overlapped. A boy couldn't walk before he'd been weaned; couldn't take a gin before his manhood had been proved. These things were done in order.

This was why the question of the girl's sex had never interested the bush boy. Didn't interest him now. For in his tribal timetable he had only arrived at the stage of walking alone: the stage immediately preceding the proving-of-manhood: the stage of the walkabout.

In the bush boy's tribe every male who reached the age of thirteen or fourteen had to perform a walk-about – a selective test which weeded out and exterminated the weaker members of the tribe, and ensured that only the fittest survived to father children. This custom is not common to all Aboriginal tribes, but is confined to the Bindaboo, the most primitive and least-known of the Aboriginal groups who live among the water-holes of the Central and North Australian desert. The test consisted of journeying from one group of water-holes to another; a journey which invariably took some six to eight months and was made entirely unaided and alone. It was a test of mental and physical toughness far fairer – but no less stringent – than the Spartan exposure of new-born babies.

It was this test that the bush boy was now engaged on. He had been doing well: had covered the most difficult part of the journey. Yet he wasn't, it seemed, to be allowed to finish it. For the lubra had looked into his eyes and seen the Spirit of Death.

Death was the Aboriginal's only enemy, his only fear. There was for him no future life: no Avalon, no Valhalla, no Islands of the Blest. That perhaps was why he watched death with such unrelaxing vigilance; that certainly was why he feared it with a terror beyond all 'civilized' comprehension. That was why he now stood in the middle of the Sturt Plain, trembling and ice-cold, his body beaded in little globules of sweat.

Peter looked in amazement, first at the bush boy then at his sister. He couldn't grasp what was happening; couldn't understand how things had gone so suddenly and terribly wrong. Afraid, his recently-acquired confidence quite drained away, he reached for his sister's hand. Then, unexpectedly, he started to cry.

To the bush boy the little one's tears were confirmation: confirmation of what the lubra had seen.

He turned away. He left the *worwora* at the edge of the billabong; he left the lace-edged panties by the ashes of last night's hearth. Slowly he walked away into the desert.

CHAPTER NINE

THE children watched him. The girl was very pale and breathing quickly. The boy was whimpering; shocked; frightened; caught up in a cross-fire of emotions he couldn't begin to understand. But one fact did penetrate the haze of his bewilderment. The bush boy, for the second time since their meeting him, was deserting them: their life-line, once again, was drifting away.

Suddenly, violently, he flung off his sister's hand and rushed stumbling into the desert.

'Hey, darkie!' His voice was frightened. 'Come back. Come back.'

The bush boy walked on: unheeding, apparently unhearing: like a sleep-walker. But Peter wouldn't be denied. Blindly he launched himself at the bush boy's legs, clutching him round the knees.

'You're not to go,' he panted.

And he hung on, like a leech.

The bush boy was jerked to a halt: was shaken out of his trance. He put his hands on the white boy's shoulders, pushing him gently away. But Peter wouldn't release his grip.

'You're not to go' – he repeated it over and over again. 'Not to go. Not to go. Not to go.'

The bush boy squatted down; so that his face was

close to the little one's; so that the little one could look into his eyes and see the terrible thing that was there. With their faces less than eighteen inches apart the two boys stared into each other's eyes.

But to the bush boy's astonishment, the little one didn't draw back; gave no exclamation of terror; seemed to see nothing wrong. He got to his feet. Puzzled. For a moment hope came surging back. Perhaps the lubra had been mistaken: perhaps the Spirit of Death had been only passing through him, resting awhile as he passed from one tribe to another: perhaps he had left him now.

He retraced his steps, back towards the girl.

But as soon as he neared her, all hope drained away. For at his approach the lubra again shrank back; in her eyes all the former terror came welling up.

The bush boy knew then that he was going to die. Not perhaps today, nor tomorrow, nor even the next day. But soon. Before the coming of the rains and the smoking of spirits out of the tribal caves. This knowledge numbed his mind, but didn't paralyse it. He was still able to think of other things. Of the queer strangers, for example – the lubra and the little one – of what would happen to them. When he died, they would die too. That was certain, for they were such helpless creatures. So there'd be not one victim for the Spirit of Death but three. Unless he could somehow save them?

Then in a moment of clarity he saw what he must do. He must lead the strangers to safety: to the final goal of his walkabout: to the valley-of-waters-under-the-earth. And they must waste no time. For who knew how much time they would have.

He gathered up the *worwora*, and smoothed out the ash of the fire.

'Kurura,' he said. And struck out across the desert.

The little one followed him at once. But the lubra didn't move. He thought for a long time that she had decided to stay by the billabongs, but in the end she too started to follow, but keeping a long way behind.

CHAPTER TEN

T HE desert was neither flat nor monotonous; nor was it like so many other deserts – the Gobi, the Steppes, or certain parts of the Sahara – featureless and devoid of colour. Its formation was varied: patches of sand, outcrops of rock, dried-up water-courses, salt-pans, faults, and frequent belts of vegetation. And its colours were strong: bold and harsh and sharply-defined: belts of yellow, blocks of bottle-green, patches of fire-flame red and fields of blood.

The bush boy led the way unhesitatingly: across the salt-pans, through the scattered yellow-jackets – poor relations to the gums – around the outcrops of quartz and granite. It was eight years since his tribe had last passed this way. He'd been little more than a toddler then; but small as he was his memory and instinct had been at work, recording landmarks, storing up information that might be of use for the future – information that was proving invaluable now.

Soon they came to a valley, gently-rising, coiling like a lifeless snake aslant a range of low granite hills. Here the country was heavily timbered: stately white-barked eucalyptus, tatty yellow-jackets, saw-leafed banksias, and occasional patches of sandalwood – source of the incense-shedding joss-sticks that smoulder beneath the images of a million oriental gods. And as the trees increased in number, so did the birds. There hadn't been many beside the hill-that-had-fallen-out-of-the-moon; but here, in the shade of the eucalyptus, they were in their thousands: gang-gangs and finches; honey-suckers and soldier-birds; budgerigars (love-birds to the romantically-minded; tiny flitting gems of mauve and olive, gold, jade-green, and cobalt-blue); and, perched on the branches of the gum trees, row after row of wonga-wongas: sad-faced, motionless, silent as the desert itself.

After the children had pushed some way into the valley, another type of bird made its presence known: a strange, sorrowful bird that followed their tracks, hopping from branch to branch with piteous, heart-rending cries.

'It isn't yours,' he wailed. 'It isn't yours.'

The children paused; looked back. At first they could see nothing. Then, with a sudden fluttering swoop, a red-breasted pardalote swept over their heads to settle on the branch of a nearby eucalyptus.

'It isn't yours. It isn't yours.' The mournful cry echoed among the leaves.

The bush boy turned to Peter, explaining by mime the pardalote's behaviour. Ahead was water – thirstily the bush boy gulped – where the bird was accustomed to drink; and he was loath to share his private reservoir with strangers. For the pardalote was a bird with an abnormal thirst; he drank eighty to a hundred times a day, and not by the normal process of imbibing through the beak, but by settling himself on top of the water, spreading his wings and absorbing liquid through the delicate membrane of his skin. No wonder he wanted to keep his pool to himself! Yet by his very loquaciousness he guided others straight to the water he sought to hide. The bush boy led on, knowing that should he take a wrong turning the pardalote's contented silence would warn him of his mistake. And soon they came to a small, fern-ringed basin, fed by an underground spring.

The pardalote, by now, had stopped his wailing. In angry silence he watched the children drinking his water, refreshing themselves at his pool.

It was midday. The sun was hot; and the boys scooped up great palmfuls of water and sloshed them over their heads. Mary too. But she wouldn't go near the bush boy; and whenever he looked at her, she shrank away.

For lunch they ate the worwora: uncooked.

During the meal Peter tried to comfort his sister: asked her what she was frightened of. But he soon gave up. She was, he decided, in one of her incomprehensible moods. Girls were like that. Sometimes the only thing to do was to leave them alone. He wandered across to the bush boy and lay down beside him, in the shade of an outcrop of rock.

They stayed by the pool for three hours, avoiding the worst of the heat; then the bush boy decided it was time they moved on. Soon they were again on their way, traversing the upper slopes of the gently-sloping valley.

That day they covered fifteen miles. The bush boy could have walked twice as far. But Peter tired easily;

and the Aboriginal adjusted his pace accordingly. Also Peter had lost his shoes – had left them together with his shirt somewhere beside the billabongs – and his feet, unused to hard going, had started to blister.

Late in the evening they came to the head of the valley, to where it petered out on the edge of a million-acre plateau. The trees were still with them, though not so thickly-growing now. So were the birds. The chat-chats, the corellas, and the sweetly-singing bellbirds; and, a little before dark, the bustards. There were three of the bustards. Foolish, inquisitive birds, rather like scraggy turkeys, they followed the children almost at their heels: sniffing, scratching, and pecking. The bush boy watched them thoughtfully, calculating their food value. One was smaller than the others: the chick: he would be tender, and plump enough to satisfy the hunger of three. Slowly, imperceptibly, the bush boy dropped behind; edging ever closer to the foolish birds. Suddenly – as if it had been thrown – his hand flew out. His fingers closed round the baby bustard's neck; cut off its life in a single twisting jerk.

Swinging his victim carelessly, the bush boy went up to the girl. Before she realized quite what was happening, he had thrust the bustard, wings and body still a-twitch, into her arms. For wasn't she a lubra: a carrier of burdens?

A drop of blood from the broken neck splashed darkly on to the girl's dress. But she didn't drop the bustard She held on to it: tightly: though her face puckered in nausea with every twitch of its wings.

Peter saw her distress.

'Say, Mary! He should'a given it to me. I'll hump it for you.'

He tried to take hold of the bird, but the girl turned away.

'It's heavy,' she whispered. 'I'll take it.'

In single file they pushed on, over the rim of the plateau; ebony silhouettes against a sunset sky.

That night they camped in a fault, a broad slab-sided rift that split the plateau like a crack in sun-dried mud. There was no water; but the rocks retained the warmth of the sun, and the twilight wind passed high over their heads.

The bush boy again made fire, though this time there was little yacca wood, and it proved more difficult to light. But by the time the sun had set flames were flickering cheerfully, their shadows duplicated on the firelit rocks of the fault; and by the time the Southern Cross had tilted up, low on the horizon, the bustard was cooking in the fire-heated ash. They would eat it, the bush boy indicated, in the morning.

As they lay down to sleep, all the day's constraint – which had ebbed somewhat away during the lighting of the fire – came flooding back. The girl kept moving about, keeping the fire between herself and the bush boy. Peter, worn out by the day's exertions, quite lost patience with her.

'Stop fidgeting, Mary!' His voice was peevish. 'I can't get to sleep.'

'Sorry, Pete.'

For a while there was silence. The bush boy moved

quietly about the camp, banking down the fire, brushing aside random splinters of wood. Watching him, the girl tossed and turned. At last she could bear it no longer.

'Peter!' Her voice was low, and somewhat different from usual. Pleading: almost frightened.

'Yes?'

'Come and lie close to me. Please.'

'What for?'

'I'm cold.'

Reluctantly he crawled across, and the two children snuggled closely together.

The girl insisted on lying with her face to the fire. From where she lay she could see the bush boy, silhouetted against the firelight; he was standing on one foot, staring into the moonlit valley. She wondered what he was thinking: wondered if he was waiting for her to fall asleep. But I won't sleep, she promised herself. Not till he does. She said it over and over again. Not till he does. Not till he does. But at last her eyes started to droop, her breathing to deepen; and a little before midnight, in spite of her resolutions, she slept the sleep of the utterly exhausted.

But the bush boy didn't sleep. Hour after hour he stood there: silent: motionless: a shadow carved in ebony and moonlight.

CHAPTER ELEVEN

PHYSICALLY the Australian Aboriginal is tough. He can stand any amount of heat, exposure, or cold; and his incidence to pain is remarkably low. But he has his Achilles Heel. Mental euthanasia. A propensity for dying purely of auto-suggestion.

Experiments have proved this: experiments carried out by Australia's leading doctors. On the one hand a group of Aboriginals – voluntarily of course – have spent a day in the desert at a temperature of roughly 95°–100° Fahrenheit, and have spent the night in a sealed-off chamber, thermostatically controlled to a temperature of minus 15° (47° of frost). They slept well without any sort of protection; and, though they were naked, felt no cold. On the other hand, Aboriginals who are a hundred per cent physically fit have been known to die purely because a tribal medicine man has put the death curse on them. One such man was admitted to a state-capital hospital. Thorough tests proved that there was nothing the matter with him; psycho-analysts tried to instil in him the will to live, the will to fight. But in vain. The medicine man had said he was going to die. And die he did: of self-induced apathy.

Death, to the Aboriginal, is something that can't

be fought. Those whom the Spirit wants, he takes; and it's no good kicking against the pricks.

That was why the bush boy accepted the fact of his impending death without question, without struggle. There was in his mind no flicker of hope. The lubra's terror, to him, could have only the one meaning. He had seen terror like hers before: in a woman's eyes after prolonged and unsuccessful child-birth; in an old man's face when he had become too weak to walk and the tribe had passed him by, leaving him alone, alone in the waterless desert. And so he now stood; without hope; passively waiting; won-dering, as he stared across the moonlit valley, how and when the Spirit of Death would come to claim him.

CHAPTER TWELVE

ALL night the bustard baked in the ashes, and by morning it was tender as broiled lamb. The children ate it hungrily.

Peter and Mary wanted to linger over the meal, would have liked to pick every succulent scrap off the bustard's bones; but the bush boy was impatient to be off. Morning mist was still clinging to the sides of the rift valley, when he smoothed out the ashes of the fire, beckoned to the others and moved off along the fault. He set a fast pace.

Mary, not knowing the cause of his hurry, wished he'd be more considerate: for Peter's sake. But, in spite of her misgivings, Peter's vitality – at least in the early morning – seemed to be limitless, quite capable of measuring up to the bush boy's long loping stride. Indeed, he apparently had energy to spare. For he hopped around the bush boy like an exuberant puppy, his shrill questioning voice echoing back from the rocks. And strangely enough the Aboriginal seemed to be understanding – and answering – his questions.

Peter had decided to learn the black boy's language – it would be far more useful than the French his sister was always boasting about. He trotted up to the Aboriginal, holding a fragment of rock.

'Say, darkie! What you call this?'

'*Garsha.*' The bush boy spoke with a grating harshness, hard as the flint itself.

'And this?' The white boy plucked at a tussock of grass.

'*Karathara.*' The word was whispered, liltingly, like the rustle of wind through a sea of grain.

'*Garsha. Karathara ... Garsha. Karathara,*' Peter's reedy treble echoed down the valley. He went rushing on ahead. Presently he came trotting back, and handed the bush boy a lump of quartz. Hour after hour the questioning went on. Mary felt very much alone.

For lunch they ate yams: queer-looking bushman-drakes that grew in dishevelled heaps beneath an out-crop of rock. Once again they rested through the midday heat – at least Mary rested; the boys chattered like gossiping kookaburras – then they were walking again, heading south-west across the red sandstone plateau.

The plateau was not a pleasant place for walking. It shimmered with heat; the children's footsteps kicked up a cloud of fine red dust, and there was no water. Soon even the ebullient Peter was reduced to a sober plod. The dust hung for a long time in the motion-less air; so that looking back the children could see behind them a winding haze of redness stretching far across the plain. After a while Peter started to sneeze. The dust was tickling his nose.

At the first sneeze the bush boy grinned (remembering their original meeting); but when the sneezing continued, becoming louder and louder as the dust inflamed Peter's nostrils, the bush boy looked at him anxiously. He hoped the little one hadn't caught the fever-that-comes-with-the-rains.

Peter, in fact, was starting nothing worse than a common cold – the type that is almost chronic among people who fly long distances and experience sudden changes in temperature – and this cold was now being aggravated by the plateau dust. He sneezed and sneezed and sneezed; he went red in the face; his eyes poured water. The bush boy regarded him with astonishment. Aboriginals know all about fever, but they never have colds and they seldom sneeze. Certainly the black boy had never witnessed such prolonged and noisy paroxysms as Peter's.

All that afternoon and half the evening the little boy sneezed his way across the dusty plain; he only stopped when they came to the edge of the plateau and the soft redstone gave way to granite; smooth and hard, not to be kicked up by shuffling feet. By the time they stopped for the night Peter was utterly exhausted: too tired to help the bush boy with fire-making: too done-in to eat. He crawled wearily across to his sister, put his head on her lap, and fell instantly asleep.

The bush boy banked down the fire. He was pleased with their progress – that day they had covered seventeen miles. If they kept to this pace, another seven sleeps would see them to the valley-of-waters-under-the-earth. Once they got there, the strangers would be safe.

He didn't go near the lubra – knowing that for some reason his nearness alarmed her (perhaps because she was ignorant enough to think that the Spirit of Death might pass, in juxtaposition, from him to her). Instead, he lay quietly down, on the opposite side of the fire.

He was just drifting into the dream-time when, quite unexpectedly, he sneezed.

*

Morning mist refracted the rays of the sun, tumbling them into the valley like a river of molten gold. Bathed in sudden light, the children stirred.

The bush boy was first to wake. He woke completely and instantly, every bit of him together: one second lost to the world, the next completely alert. He rose, flexed his muscles, sniffed the air, and walked quietly down-valley.

Peter woke next. He sat up yawning, rubbing eyes and nose. He'd have liked to blow his nose really (it felt all bunged-up) but having no handkerchief, he sniffed. Loudly.

His sister rolled on to her side and looked at him critically.

'Peter.' Her voice was disapproving. 'Where's your hanky?'

'Lost.'

He didn't wait for recriminations, but got up quickly.

'I'm going to look for the darkie. Coming?'

She shook her head, and lay down again. He wondered why she looked suddenly hurt: as though he'd slapped her across the face.

He wandered off; hands in pockets, sniffing loudly.

Instinctively he headed down the valley, down the broad granite cleft that ran like an axe-cut from plateau-rim to fringe of plain. He had been too tired the night before to take notice of their camp site – it had been simply a place to go to sleep in; but now, the scenery's bizarre grandeur caught his imagination. It was, he decided, just like the moon: just like those rocky, fierce-coloured lunar landscapes of the comic strips. He peered at the rocks a little apprehensively, half-expecting some Martian monster to come leaping out; indeed, from the far side of a jagged outcrop of granite, he could, now that he listened carefully, hear something that sounded rather like a Martian feeding: a sort of scrunching-mingled-with-heavy-breathing noise. Fear fought curiosity, and lost. Cautiously he squirmed his way up the wall of rocks, and peered over the edge.

Twenty feet below him was a small pool, rock-ringed, crystal clear, and motionless as glass. And beside it was the bush boy, trundling a small boulder of quartz, about the size of a football (but ten times its weight). He saw Peter and grinned.

'*Yarrawa!*' He pointed to the pool.

Peter glissaded down. He saw the *yarrawa* at once. Fish. Silver-scaled, glistening, darting; ranging in size from three to fifteen inches; on their sides a row of small black dots, like the port-holes of a liner. He suddenly remembered that he'd had no breakfast.

'*Yeemara?*' He pointed at the fish.

The bush boy nodded.

The pool was shallow at one end, and Peter waded

in. He could see the fish quite clearly; there were thousands of them – well, hundreds, anyhow – but whenever his hand snaked down to clutch them, they darted away. Like quicksilver. The bush boy laughed. He beckoned Peter out of the pool, and led him to a smooth circular rock, smaller than his, but quite as heavy, he suspected, as the little one could lift.

'*Kurura,*' he said. And started to trundle his boulder of quartz up to a shelving ledge of rock that overhung the pool. Peter followed him; and soon the boys and their stones were poised on the edge of the rock that jutted out, like a diving-board, over the water. The bush boy mimed his intention. Peter nodded in understanding; and together they hoisted up their boulders, staggered with them to the lip of the rock and hurled them into the pool. The splash was cataclysmic, loud as a whip-crack, echoing round the encircling rock; the spray was torrential, like the collapsing of a miniature waterspout; and the concussion, in the confined, rock-bound pool, was overwhelming, like the explosion of a depth-charge. The fish were stunned: upside-down they came floating to the surface.

The bush boy leapt into the pool. Peter followed. Together, they grabbed at the paralysed fish, tossing them out of the water, on to the rocks. Within sixty seconds a couple of dozen *yarrawa* were squirming their lives out, on the smooth, sun-hot granite.

The bush boy was jubilant. Climbing out of the pool, he gathered the fish together, in a twisting, glistening heap, playing with them, trickling them through his fingers like a miser worshipping his gold.

There were so many fish and they were so slippery, that when the boys wanted to take them back to the camp site they couldn't carry them. Not until Peter took off his shorts. Then, in these, they wrapped the *yarrawa* up, and carried them back in triumph.

When the children had eaten – three fish apiece – Peter refused to put on his shorts. There was quite a scene.

'Feel them,' the little boy said. 'They're horrid and scaly. Full of fish.'

'Wash them, and put them on,' his sister ordered.

'Shan't!'

Peter eyed her defiantly.

It was the bush boy who settled the argument. He was ready to move again; the *yarrawa* were too valuable to be left behind; he rolled them up in the little one's shorts and tossed the bundle to the lubra.

'*Kurura,*' he said.

And so they began the fourth day of the walkabout.

The going was easier than on the plateau: down the lower reaches of the valley then out across the plain – the vast, lonely, and limitless plain that rolled on and on, a flowering wilderness, silent as sleep, motionless as death.

Over the level ground the bush boy moved quickly. Too quickly for Peter, whose cold made him short of breath. Soon the little boy was panting. After a couple of hours his nose started to stream. The midday halt – in the shade of a group of golden casuarinas – was never more welcome. But it only lasted a couple of hours. Then they were walking again. Across the endless plain. On and on.

Half-way through the afternoon, as they were crossing a monotonous belt of scrub, there came a diversion: as welcome as it was unexpected. The children were walking in their usual order – the bush boy first, Peter next, Mary in the rear – when suddenly the bush boy stopped: stopped dead: like a pointer, one foot off the ground, nose forward, an arm flung behind him for balance. For perhaps half a minute he stayed motionless: frozen; then he crept quietly forward, to where a low bank of wattle-bush formed a screen of scarlet around a tiny clearing. Expectantly the others joined him. Together they peered through the wattle leaves.

They saw a bird. An ordinary rather sad-looking bird, with big eyes, pointed beak and long, straggling tail. He was scratching about for grubs. To the white children the scene looked very prosaic: an anti-climax. But the black boy was obviously enthralled; he signalled to them to be quiet, and so they knelt close up to the wattle-bushes: motionless: expectant. And after about ten minutes their patience was rewarded.

Quite suddenly the bird raised his head; he drew himself erect and, with a stiff-legged goose-step, strutted into the centre of the clearing. Then he started to sing. And in an instant all his drabness was sloughed away. For his song was beautiful beyond compare: stream after stream of limpid melodious notes, flowing and mingling, trilling and soaring:

bush music, magic as the pipes of Pan. On and on it went; wave after wave of perfect harmony that held the children spellbound. At last the notes sank into a croon, died into silence. The song was over. But not the performance. For now came a metamorphosis too amazing to be believed. The drab brown bird with its tatty, straggling tail disappeared, and in its place rose a creature of pure beauty. The drooping tail fanned wide; its two outmost feathers swung erect to form the frame of a perfect lyre; and in between spread a mist of elfin plumage, a phantasmagoria of blue and silver, shot with gold, that trembled and quivered with all the beauty of a rainbow seen through running water. Then, hidden behind his plumage, the lyre bird again burst into song. And as he sang, he danced; prancing joyfully from side to side, hopping and skipping to the beat of a high-speed polka. And every now and then his song broke off, was interspersed with croaking chuckles of happiness.

Then, as suddenly as his performance had begun, it ended. The feathers drooped, the polka came to a halt, the singing died. And he was just another bird, scratching the earth for food.

The children walked on. The sun dropped lower. The western sky glowed rose and gold.

At the first breath of the sunset wind they made camp beside a group of eucalyptus. There was no water; but the fish alleviated their thirst.

Out of the dusk came ants: winged ants: flying in swarms: attracted by the glow of the fire. Mating in mid-air they shed their wings, dropping inter-twined to earth. The bush boy stirred up the flames to move them on. Coils of wood-smoke streamed downwind.

Peter moved farther away from the fire – for the smoke brought tears to his eyes, brought on another attack of sneezing. But his sneezes were neither as prolonged nor as violent as they'd been the night before. For his cold was on the mend. Though they'd again walked close on fifteen miles, he felt reasonably fresh: fresh enough, at any rate, to appreciate the miming.

For now, out of the shadows and into the firelight, strutted the bush boy. In his hands were three leafy branchlets. These he draped about his body, to represent wings and tail. Then he started to dance: to mimic the polka-ing lyre bird. Round and round the fire he strutted, pantomimed, and pranced; then he screwed up his mouth and burst into shrill, raucous singing. His absurdities grew more tempestuous, more abandoned, yet never lost their realism.

At first the white children were simply amused. Then, as the pantomime grew even livelier, even more grotesque, their amusement turned to unrestrained delight. They laughed and laughed, till the leaves fell from the humble-bushes; they stamped their feet and clapped their hands, till the floor of the desert seemed to shake, and sparks from the fire went whirling away, like fairy lanterns, into the night.

Then, suddenly and unexpectedly, in the middle of his dance, the bush boy sneezed. He sneezed again and again and again (as he'd never sneezed before). Abruptly the pantomiming came to an end.

The sneezing had a curious effect on the bush boy. He seemed to grow suddenly weak. He passed a hand over his forehead, and his fingers came away damp. When he saw this dampness a great fear came over him. He remembered an old man he'd seen in the tribal caves: an old man who had sneezed at the time of the rains, whose forehead had become damp with fever, whose body had been very light when they'd lifted it on to its burial platform. He began to tremble. Slowly, uncertainly, he walked across to the fire. He lay close beside it; close to its warmth; but he couldn't stop shivering.

The white children looked at the bush boy in astonishment. But neither went to him: the boy because in the last few days he'd witnessed so many incomprehensible changes of mood he'd come to disregard them; the girl for reasons of her own. Soon both brother and sister slept. But the bush boy didn't sleep. Not for many hours. He lay close to the warmth of the fire, but he couldn't stop trembling. And quite frequently he sneezed.

CHAPTER THIRTEEN

I T was obvious, next morning, that the bush boy
had caught Peter's cold. His nose was running, his
eyes were heavy, his muscles ached. Long after sunrise he was still sitting beside the dying fire, too lethar-
gic apparently to think of breakfast. Peter and Mary
tidied up the camp, replenished the fire, cooked the
last of the *yarrawa* and offered the bush boy a share –
but he wouldn't eat. Then they waited: waited for
him to move.

But he just went on sitting; hour after hour.

'Say, Mary!' The little boy was worried. 'I guess
he's ill.'

'He looks O.K. to me.'

'Reckon I'll ask him.'

Peter went up to the bush boy.

'Hey, darkie! You O.K.?' He eyed him anxiously.
' 'Cause if you are, let's get shiftin' for Adelaide.'

The bush boy blinked: came suddenly out of his
trance. He saw the lubra and the little one looking at
him anxiously, and remembered that the valley-of-
waters-under-the-earth was still five sleeps away. He
got to his feet. Slowly. And without a word struck
southward, through the scrub.

All that morning they walked in silence.

A little after noon the bush boy started to cast

around, as if unsure of the trail. Twenty-four hours ago he'd have explained to Peter what he was looking for; but he was too preoccupied now. He soon found what he wanted: the claw marks of a food-searching bird. He followed the marks up, picking out a trail that the white children never even saw: a trail of toe-scratchings, odd feathers, and droppings: a trail that led at last to a circular hillock, three feet high: a hillock built by the talegulla (bush turkey) out of earth and decomposing leaves. Inside the hillock, the bush boy knew, would be eggs: the eggs of the bush-turkey: the fowl that knows no broodiness: that lays its eggs and wanders off, leaving the warmth of the decomposing leaves to hatch its deserted offspring.

There were fourteen eggs in the mound, each partitioned off from its neighbours by walls of decaying leaves. One by one the bush boy unearthed them: steaming, pink-tinted, and the size of golf balls. The children roasted and ate them. The firm, nut-flavoured flesh was nourishing; it satisfied their hunger, but sharpened their thirst. Of water there was no sign.

The midday rest was longer than usual; and once again the white children had to coerce the bush boy into making a start. His cold was coming out now; his nose was streaming, his eyes were heavy, his sneezes were interspersed by an occasional cough. When at last he did start off, his pace was slow: as if every step was an effort.

Peter tried to cheer him up, but without success. The Aboriginal had gone into a semi-trance; he moved like a sleep-walker: lost in a world of his own.

'Say, Mary!' The little boy was worried. 'He ain't well. You do something.'

'He's just got a cold, Pete. Like you had. Nothing to fuss about.'

'But look at his eyes. They're all queer an' starey.'

But the girl wouldn't look at the bush boy's eyes.

'He's O.K.,' she said. 'Don't fuss.'

They walked all afternoon, all evening, and a little way into the night – for the first water-hole they came to had dried up. In the second well the water was brackish and faintly salt, but the children drank it: greedily.

The bush boy wasn't going to bother over a fire; but Peter and Mary, tired as they were, collected wood, and persuaded the Aboriginal to help them get it alight. Then the three of them, utterly exhausted, lay down to sleep. Peter dropped off at once; Mary after a little while; but the bush boy stayed awake, hour after hour. He felt hot one minute and cold the next. Convinced that he was getting the fever-that-comes-with-the-rains, he kept feeling his forehead. And a little after midnight his fingers came away damp. He started to tremble then. He hoped the lubra and the little one knew how to make a burial platform: high off the ground: so that the evil spirits couldn't creep out and start to molest his body.

*

Next day the sun had risen high before the children were on the move. They had no breakfast, and the bush boy was noticeably weaker. But at last they started off, heading south by west across the level plain. In the distance, heat-hazed and very far away, they could see a low range of hills. The bush boy pointed to the hills.

'Arkooloola,' he said.

And that was the only word he spoke until their midday rest.

But a little before noon he came – if only for a moment – out of his lethargy.

It was Peter who saw the echidna first: a pair of porcupine-like creatures scurrying between two clumps of yacca. He grabbed the bush boy's hand.

'Look! Food! Yeemara!'

The bush boy came suddenly to life. He snapped off a branch of yacca, and leapt after the echidna. They heard him coming; they tried to escape in the only manner they knew; by diving under the ground; by burrowing into the earth as if it were chocolate marshmallow. But the bush boy was too quick for them. With a thrust of the yacca he blocked their getaway; with the end of the branch he prised them up to the surface. He unrolled them, skilfully avoiding their quills, and set them down on the sand. In the pouch of the female he found a tiny replica of herself: a frightened, blinking pup, whose quills were soft as chickens' down. Gently he put the mother down; set her free to tend her young; to raise the pup to a size more suitable for food. But for the male there was no reprieve. His death blow was mercifully swift; his body was tossed to the lubra. They ate him, when the

83

day was at its hottest, casseroled in eucalyptus leaves.

For a long time that afternoon the hills seemed to come no nearer; then, quite suddenly, the children were walking into their shadow.

They found an idyllic place to camp; in the shade of an outcrop of rocks and close to a stream that meandered into a looping chain of billabongs. They drank deeply, kindled their fire and settled down in the shade of a boxwood thicket for the night.

The bush boy's cold didn't appear to be any worse; indeed if anything he was sneezing and coughing less. Yet he seemed weaker: increasingly preoccupied: and the children noticed that his coordination was beginning to fail – twice, while making fire, the yacca rolled from between his hands.

Peter was very solicitous. Seeing the bush boy huddled by the fire yet still trembling – he supposed with cold – he took off his shorts and tried to cover him up. And the Aboriginal seemed to be grateful. Peter looked at him thoughtfully: then at his sister. He had a sudden idea.

'Hey, Mary!' His cheerful shout echoed back from the rocks. 'The darkie's cold. Couldn't he have your dress?'

The girl's mouth fell open. For a second she stared at her brother in disbelief. Then she swung round and started to bank up the fire.

But the little boy wasn't put off.

'Gee, Mary! Don't be a meany. He's cold.'

The girl said nothing.

Peter looked at her curiously. Her face had gone suddenly pale; her eyes, once again, were frightened, hunted.

'I think you're scared!' the little boy announced with unexpected relish. 'Cowardy girl! Cowardy girl.'

Mary turned away. She hid her face in her hands. If only he wasn't so small; if only he was a few years older; then he'd understand.

She saw the bush boy looking at her: watching her. And she shivered.

The Southern Cross blazed out of a cobalt sky; the sundown wind faded to a whisper; and a pair of marsupial rats, their eyes aglow like luminous peas, hopped hesitantly round the camp site. Mary threw a branch of yacca into the flames. The sparks crackled and flew; and the rats, with tiny ping-ponging hops, fled. The stars glowed like gems. The desert, and the children, slept.

*

Next morning Peter woke early. He yawned; stretched; looked first at the others – still asleep – then at the billabongs. The water looked cool and tempting. He got up, strolled across to the nearest pool, sat on the edge and dangled in an exploratory toe. The water was delightfully warm; but shallow; barely up to his knees. He wandered upstream, seeking a deeper, more exciting pool.

He found it on the far side of the outcrop of rock: a

granite-encircled basin, fed by a miniature waterfall. With a noisy belly-flop, he dived in.

The pool was exactly the right depth: up to his armpits. Working his way to under the waterfall, he revelled in the cascading, sunlit spray. He stayed a long time in the water, soaking every pore of his sturdy young body. He noticed with satisfaction that his body wasn't white any longer; a week's continual exposure to the desert sun had tanned it a rich mahogany – only he hoped it wouldn't get any darker, else he'd be turning into a blackamoor. At last he wandered back to the camp site.

The bush boy was still asleep; but Mary had just woken, and he told her about the rock-bound billabong.

The girl looked at the Aboriginal and saw that he was motionless: apparently fast asleep.

'You stir up the fire, Pete,' she said. 'Can you manage that? While I bathe?'

'Sure I can manage.'

She smiled, glad of his self-reliance, and made her way to the far side of the rock.

The billabong was everything Peter had promised. The river that ran out of Eden couldn't have been more beautiful. The girl took off her dress, ruefully noting its rents and tears, shook loose her hair, and dived into the pool. The water was crystal clear and warm as a tepid bath. Lazily she swam across to the waterfall, and let the spray cascade on to her naked body. She felt relaxed, washed clean of cares and doubts and fears. Sometime, she thought, some distant day or week or month, they'd come to Adelaide (or some other settlement); the bush boy she wouldn't think about; in the meantime the sun shone, there was water to drink, food to eat, and Peter's cold was on the mend. She started to sing: gaily: swirling her hair from shoulder to shoulder.

Peter, meanwhile, had fanned the fire into a blazing pyre of yacca. And the bush boy had woken up.

He lay on his back, thinking. He wasn't used to thinking – most of his actions being dictated by custom and instinct rather than thought. But there was something he had to think about now: something vitally important: his burial table. Did the strangers know how to make it: high off the ground: so that the serpent that slept in the bowels of the earth couldn't creep out and molest his body? The strangers were such an ignorant pair; he couldn't leave anything to chance; he'd have to make sure they knew what had to be done.

He got to his feet. Slowly. Weakly.

If other things had been equal he'd have talked to the little one – he was on easier terms with him than with the lubra. But he saw that the little one was working: was collecting firewood; while the lubra, to judge from her singing and splashing, was merely washing her body. Tribal custom frowned on disturbing those who were working. And it never occurred to the bush boy to wait for a more propitious moment. He set off to find the lubra.

He climbed the outcrop of rock and saw her a little way below him, bathing in the billabong. She'd taken off her strange decorations, and loosened her hair so that it was no longer scraped up on the back of her head but flowed, long and golden, on the surface of the water. The bush boy had never seen such hair, sand-coloured and trailing like the comet that rides the midnight sky. He thought it very beautiful. He lay down on the sun-warmed rock, and stared. Admiringly.

Quite suddenly the girl looked up: looked up straight into his eyes: into his staring, admiring eyes.

She backed away. In terror. Her hands, sliding along the bank of the pool, clutched at a loosened fragment of rock. She pulled the rock free; grasped it firmly.

The bush boy came walking down to the billabong. But at the water's edge he stopped: stopped in amazement. For the lubra was snarling at him; was snarling like a cornered dingo, her nose wrinkled, her lips curled back, her eyes filled with terror. He took a hesitant step forward, saw the stone in the lubra's hand and stopped again. Hatred was something alien to the bush boy; but he couldn't fail to recognize the look in the lubra's eyes. He knew, in that moment, that his body would never get its burial platform.

He felt suddenly weaker: much weaker. Things were happening that he didn't understand: didn't want to understand. He looked at the lubra's frightened eyes and snarling mouth, and was appalled. The will to live drained irrevocably away.

Slowly he turned. He walked a few paces back into the desert; then he lay down in the shade of a mugga-wood tree.* The branches hung limply over him; the great puce-coloured flowers wept their tears of blood.

* The mugga-wood, to the Aboriginals, is the tree of sorrow, symbol of the broken heart; for its appearance is sad and drooping, and its flowers are perpetually wet with a crimson fluid, seeping out like blood.

CHAPTER FOURTEEN

THE yacca wood burned quickly, and Peter had a full-time job replenishing the fire. He couldn't think what was keeping the others; but he hoped they'd come soon – before he ran out of firewood.

At last he saw his sister scrambling down the out-crop of rock. Even from a distance he sensed that something was wrong; and when she came slowly up to the fire and held out her hands to the blaze, he noticed about her an unnatural calm, an air of too carefully imposed restraint. For a while neither spoke; then the girl picked up a branch and started to draw ash over the flames.

'Hey!' Peter was indignant. 'You'll put it out.'

She nodded. 'We don't need it.'

'Course we need it. How we going to cook for breakfast?'

'There's no breakfast.'

She followed the point up.

'Listen, Peter,' she moved closer to him. 'There's no food here. It's no use staying. Let's push off.'

He eyed her suspiciously.

'What's the rush? The darkie'll get food.'

'Listen, Pete' – she was pleading now – 'Let's go by ourselves. Just you an' me. We'll be O.K.'

His mouth started to droop.

'I don't wanna leave the darkie.'

'He doesn't want to come, Pete. I know he doesn't. I asked him.'

'You sure? Cross your heart.'

'Real sure. Cross my heart.'

He eyed her doubtfully: unconvinced.

'How d'you ask him? You can't talk darkie talk!'

She went on raking over the ash.

'I tell you,' she said, 'he doesn't want to come. I know.'

A week ago he'd have accepted her word; have fallen in with her plans. But not now.

'I'm goin' ask him myself.' He strode off purposefully, heading for the outcrop of rock.

The girl made as if to run after him, to pull him back. Then she stopped; that, she realized, would do no good. She sat down, beside the dead fire. Her fingers plucked at the hem of her skirt.

After about ten minutes Peter came running back; out of breath.

'Say, Mary!' his voice was frightened. 'The darkie's ill. Real ill. He's lying under a bush. An' he won't move.'

'P'raps he's asleep.'

Peter looked at her in disgust.

'Course he's not asleep. He's ill. You come an' look.'

'No!'

The girl drew back.

'No!' she whispered. 'I won't go near him.'

*

They spent a miserable, frustrating day. Peter wouldn't leave the bush boy; Mary wouldn't go near him; and they had no food.

A little before noon the white boy went wandering off upstream, and his sister followed.

'Where you going, Pete?'

'I'm gonna look for fish.'

She came with him eagerly, hoping this was the first step in breaking away, in going off on their own. But Peter wouldn't go far: after less than an hour he turned back, insisted on retracing their steps. They found no fish.

Peter spent most of the afternoon carrying palmfuls of water up from the billabong to where the bush boy lay motionless in the shade of the mugga-wood. At first the Aboriginal wouldn't drink, but eventually he accepted a little – though Peter noticed he seemed to have difficulty in swallowing.

A couple of hours before sundown the white children went on another food hunt. This time downstream. And, more by luck than judgement, they found a cluster of the yams-with-foliage-under-the-ground. They rooted up three apiece and carried them back to the camp. After a good deal of difficulty they re-kindled the fire, and covered the yams with ash. An hour later they were eating them, while the sunset wind rustled the boxwoods, and flying phalangers zoomed from tree to tree.

Peter took one of the yams to the bush boy; but he wouldn't eat.

He seemed to be much weaker; to have lost all interest in what was happening around him. Yet his cold was certainly no worse, and all trace of fever had vanished. He simply lay there, his dark eyes becoming slowly more clouded, his body temperature gradually falling, and his pulse growing imperceptibly weaker. Resigned to the inevitable, he was willing himself to death.

For a long while that evening Peter sat beside him, holding his hand. There had always been a bond between the two boys – a mutual liking and understanding – and it was because of this that Peter now realized the bush boy was dying. He held his hand more tightly. After a while he noticed the bush boy's lips; they were moving. He bent closer.

'Arkooloola!' The whisper was unmistakable.

Peter ran down to the billabong, cupped his hands, and brought back water. But the bush boy pushed it aside; he shook his head; with an effort he raised himself up.

'Arkooloola.' He pointed at Peter.

'Me?' The little boy was astonished. 'I don't wanna drink.'

'Arkooloola,' the bush boy insisted. 'Yeemara.' He pointed first at Peter then at the hills.

It was some time before the white boy cottoned on; only when the Aboriginal scooped together a ridge in the sand to represent the hills, and traced a trail from one side to the other, did he get the gist of the message. Then he nodded. Gratefully.

'Sure, darkie. I get you. Over the hills there's food

an' water, *Arkooloola* an' *yeemara*. That's fine. Now you lie down.'

The bush boy's eyes clouded over. He rolled on to his side, drew up his knees, and lay very still.

Peter took his hand; squeezed it reassuringly. Then, struck by a sudden thought, he got up and walked across to his sister.

She was sitting beside the fire – about two hundred yards from the mugga-wood – drawing patterns in the sand with a pointed branch. She looked up as Peter approached.

'How is he?'

Peter was very matter of fact.

'I guess he'll soon be dead.'

'Oh, no! No. No. No.'

She started to sway backward and forward, her hands over her face.

Her brother eyed her critically. Then he remembered what he'd come to ask.

'Say, Mary! You reckon he'll go to heaven?'

'I don't believe you.' The girl's voice was muffled. 'He's only got a cold.'

'I reckon he won't go to heaven. 'Cause he's a little heathen. He's not baptized.'

The girl got up: quickly. She started to pace up and down.

'You sure he's real ill, Pete?'

'Course I'm sure. You come an' see.'

For a long time the girl was silent. Then she said slowly:

'Yes. I'll come.'

They walked across to the mugga-wood: to where the bush boy lay in a pool of shadow. Beside him, the girl dropped hesitantly to her knees. She looked into his face: closely: and saw that what her brother had told her was true.

She sat down. Stunned. Then very gently she eased the bush boy's head on to her lap; very softly she began to run her fingers over and across his forehead.

The bush boy's eyes flickered open; for a moment they were puzzled; then they smiled.

It was the smile that broke Mary's heart: that last forgiving smile. Before, she had seen as through a glass darkly, but now she saw face to face. And in that moment of truth all her inbred fears and inhibitions were sponged away, and she saw that the world which she had thought was split in two was one.

*

He died in the false dawn: peacefully and without struggle: in the hour when the desert is specially still and the light is specially clear.

The girl didn't know when he died. For she had fallen asleep. Her head had drooped, until her cheek rested on his, and her long golden hair lay tumbled about his face.

CHAPTER FIFTEEN

THEY buried him close to the billabong.

The little boy was surprisingly matter-of-fact and practical; he insisted on the Aboriginal being christened at the same time as he was buried – 'otherwise he mightn't get to heaven'. Mary said nothing. She had a vague idea that it was too late for christening now; but that was something her brother need never know.

It was noon before they had finished – for the desert sand was hard to dig with boxwood branches and sharp-edged stones – and the children were tired and hungry. They had two yams left over from the night before, and these they ate: raw. Then they sat in the shade of the boxwoods and looked at each other.

It was Peter who took command. After a while he got to his feet.

'Come on, Mary,' he said. '*Kurura!*'

'Where to?'

'Over the hills, of course.'

The girl looked doubtful.

'You sure that's the way, Pete?'

'Sure I'm sure. The darkie told me. Over the hills there's food an' water.'

'All right,' she said. 'Let's go.'

They started to follow the stream: the clear pellucid

stream that tumbled down from the hills in alternate rapids, waterfalls and pools. All afternoon they kept close to its banks. And the ghost of the bush boy was with them in every passing plant and stone. For both children had fallen into his ways. They walked now with the bush boy's easy, distance-eating lope; their eyes – like his – were ever questing ahead, studying the terrain, picking out the most promising leads; and every now and then – as he had done – they plucked and ate the pea-sized water-containing pods that dangled from the straggling belts of bush violet: nature's thirst quenchers. It was the same that evening, when, an hour before sundown, they made camp. His ghost was in the yacca wood they picked for their fire; in the sun-warmed desert stones they chose for their hearth; in the roots of the wondilla grass and stalks of sugar cane they ate for supper. They lived as he had lived. Like his shadows. Adaptable as adults could never be, they made the desert their home.

They hadn't mentioned the bush boy during the day; but now, with the flames a-flicker and the stars aglow, they missed him more; missed him with an added poignancy. Peter looked at the Southern Cross, aflame like the jewelled hilt of a sword.

'Mary,' he whispered. 'Is heaven way up there? Way up beyond the stars?'

'That's right, Peter.'

'You reckon the darkie's there?'

'Yes, Pete. I reckon he is.'

She said it automatically: to comfort her brother. But in the same moment that she said it, suddenly and unexpectedly, she believed it. More than believed it. Knew it. Knew that heaven, like earth, was one.

*

When the children woke next morning they were hungry – they had had no meat in the last thirty-six hours, nothing more solid than vegetables and nuts. Mary woke first. She stirred the fire, tossed on a fresh supply of yacca wood, then went wandering down to the stream in search of fish.

A little above their camp, the stream widened out to form a shallow, mud-banked pool. It looked a likely place for fishing, and the girl approached it warily. A few yards short of the bank she stopped: listened. The sound of splashing was unmistakable: loud and playful. She crept forward and peered cautiously through the rushes.

In the centre of the pool three of the strangest creatures were playfully gambolling over the water. The girl looked at them in amazement – they might have come from another world – then she ran noiselessly back to fetch her brother.

Soon the two children were watching the platypus at play.

There were three of them: mother, father, and half-grown child. The adults were about twenty inches long; four-footed, fur-covered, and with enormous duck-like beaks. They were aquatic mammals – a link with the prehistoric past – web-footed egglayers; teatless milk producers – the lactic fluid being exuded through the female's skin pores; poison-fanged amphibians, with fangs in the hollow of the male's hind feet. No wonder the children stared in amazement!

Normally the platypus were timid creatures, inordinately shy; but now, confident that they were unobserved, they dived, leap-frogged, and darted about with gay agility. Then quite suddenly, quicker than sight, they vanished; for Peter, edging forward to improve his view, had trodden on and snapped a twig. It was a very small snap – the children never even heard it – but in a flash the platypus dived: dived deep: went snaking through underwater entrances to their burrow beneath the bank. There, in the maze of their smooth, highly-polished tunnels, they were safe.

The little boy looked at his sister.

'Reckon they're O.K. to eat?'

'Oh, Pete! I couldn't! Besides, we'd never catch them.'

They agreed to forgo breakfast in favour of a swim.

Peter jumped feet-first into the pool. After a while he started to mimic the platypus. He pursed out his lips, quacked and bobbed and splashed, showering his sister with spray, driving her laughing on to the bank. His miming became more hilarious, more abandoned – shades of the bush boy and lyre bird – until at last the girl joined in. Together they squawked and splashed to exhaustion; then they lay on the bank side by side in the drying warmth of the sun.

But they couldn't, Peter knew, stay by the pool for ever. And soon they were on their way, following the course of the stream, climbing the gently-rising valley.

At first the valley was well-shaded and softly-coloured: aglow with the gold of casuarinas, the creamy white of bamberas and the pink of gums and eucalyptus. But as the children climbed higher, the vegetation gradually became more stunted and the colours harsher, cruder. By midday they were traversing a rocky barren terrain, its only trees the drooping mugga-woods, its only flowers the everlasting daisies: the flowers that never die; that live on, even after their petals, leaves, stalks, and roots have crumbled and withered away. The children grew hotter, tireder, and hungrier. It was lucky that Mary had had the foresight to gather a cache of bauble nuts, and these they ate, soon after midday, in the shade of a slab of rock that overhung the stream.

The stream had become a good deal smaller by now; and looking up-valley the children could guess at its source, in a shallow cwm about two hundred feet above them. Mary looked at the hills, shading her eyes against the glare of the sun.

'Sure you know the way, Pete?'

'Course I'm sure. The darkie told me. Over the hills.'

The girl said nothing. The hills, she knew, were higher than they looked. And they'd soon be losing the stream. She wished they had something in which to carry water.

They rested for a couple of hours, then pushed on.

The valley became barer, bleaker, progressively less inviting. Yet even here, in its upper reaches, it had a certain beauty; not its former beauty of woods and shades and gentle colours; but a bold, bizarre beauty; a kaleidoscope of strange pigments and exciting, unexpected contrasts. Soon the valley slopes fanned out, exposing new vistas: wider horizons: the whole range of the hills, startlingly detailed in the clear, hazeless air. Dead ahead there swelled up a smooth, symmetrical hummock, its slopes, flecked with mica, reflecting the sun like a massed array of heliographs. To the left rose a rugged mound of granite, smooth and scalloped as a magnified Dartmoor tor. While to the right towered a fantastic pyramid of wine-veined quartz: alternate layers of crimson, grey, and black.

The children moved slowly forward; dwarfed by the immensity of the hills.

A couple of hours before sundown they came to the cwm; and here, in the saucer-shaped depression between the slopes of mica and quartz, they made camp. It wasn't a very inviting camp-site, being boggy and devoid of shade, but at least they were close to water – of a kind. They had hoped the source of the stream would be a cool, refreshing trickle filtering out of the rock; instead it turned out to be a brackish, stagnant pool, its surface filmed by the oil of decomposing leaves. For a long time the children regarded it with silent disgust. Then the ghost of the bush boy came to their aid.

'Say, Pete,' the girl had a sudden thought. 'Remember that pool way back in the salt-pan. Remember how the darkie sucked up water with a reed. We can do that.'

They searched for and found a couple of hollow

reeds: reeds of the watermat grass. Mary remembered to plug one end with moss (as a filter); then they plunged the reeds deeply into the pool, and sucked. The water they drew up was clean and cool.

Their thirst was slaked. Their hunger remained.

It was Peter who, purely by luck, solved the food problem. He was idly stirring the pool with his watermat reed – and dragging all sorts of leaf-mould and water plant to the surface – when he noticed a queer little prawn-like creature clambering out of the stirred-up water.

'Hey, Mary! There's food in the pool.'

The girl came running. Eagerly. But when she saw the 'food' she wasn't impressed.

'He's awfu' small, Pete. And all arms and legs.'

'Maybe there's other ones.'

Together they peered into the brackish water, but saw nothing.

'Say, Mary!' – it was Peter's turn to think back now – ' 'Member how the darkie killed all them fish. Throwing stones. Couldn't we do that?'

'No good here, Pete. Stones would go squelch in the mud.'

They stared disconsolately at the pool. Then the girl hit on the answer.

'I know. Let's stir up the mud. Anything in the pool will get all choked. Will have to climb out.'

It worked like a charm; better than they had dared to hope. They collected a couple of branches, plunged them into the pool, and churned up the mud. In seconds the water took on the consistency of soup:

thick soup; brown and heavy: creamed with mud and scum. And almost at once the yabbies – diminutive crayfish of the bush – came bobbing up to the surface. Choked and blinded, they fled their mud-bed haunts; desperately, like drowning men, they struggled for the bank. Bedraggled, they hauled themselves up – out of the frying-pan into the fire. For on the banks the children were waiting for them. They snatched them up; smashed their heads against the earth; killing them instantly. On and on the slaughter went, till a full three dozen yabbies (each between four and eight inches long) lay dead beside the pool.

It was Mary who called a halt.

'That's enough, Pete. Let's not kill any more.'

The yabbies, roasted on fire-heated stones, made a delicious meal. The children ate their fill, and still had enough left over for breakfast.

Soon, curled close together, they settled down for the night.

It was cooler in the hills, and they were glad of the warmth of the fire. The girl had dragged up an extra large supply of branches; and from these she picked out a couple of arm-thick trunks, and tossed them on to the fire. The sparks flew skyward; wreaths of wood-smoke drifted across the stars; down-valley a dingo howled at the crescent moon. Charleston was in another world.

*

They woke cold and coated with dew; but the resurrected fire warmed them quickly, and a breakfast of yabbies put them in good heart. They collected another two dozen of the crayfish out of the pool – for the way ahead looked barren and devoid of food – then, Peter leading, they hit off across the hills, skirting the pyramid of wine-veined quartz.

The hills had a primeval grandeur. They had been old when the Himalayas were first folded out of the level plain. Their rocky slopes were hard; enduring; unchanging from aeon to aeon. The children traversed them slowly: ants on a gargantuan tableau.

In the clear, hazeless light distances and angles were hard to judge. Slopes that looked an easy ten minutes' stroll turned out to be an hour's exhausting climb. And always at the top of one rise was another: wave after wave of swelling hillocks, always steepening, always climbing; never dropping away, never falling into the longed-for valley.

In silence the children plodded on, watched by blue-wrens and moffets that tucked their pin-thin legs beneath them and scooted about the flattened rocks like mice on inset wheels.

Soon the rocks became increasingly rugged and broken, cut into lopsided rifts and faults, as though a giant with an axe had used the hill-top as a random chopping-block. Among the faults strange colours glinted: the dull crimson of garnets, the yellow flame of topaz, the white of moonstone, and, very occasionally, the fleck of blue-green beryl. Unmined wealth. A jeweller's shop of semi-precious gems; undiscovered; unexploited.

The girl's fingers ran round the base of a moonstone.

'They're beautiful, Pete. Let's take some with us.'

'Come on, Mary. We can't eat stones.'

Reluctantly she followed her brother among the desiccated rocks. But the jewels were something she didn't forget.

Then, quite suddenly, as the children rounded a shoulder of granite, they stopped: stopped dead in disbelief. For in front of them rose a whole hillside aglow with shimmering colour: every shade of the spectrum sparkling, flickering, and interchanging: a kaleidoscope of brilliance rioting in the midday sun.

Mary's eyes widened, her mouth fell open.

'Jewels, Peter! Jewels! Millions and millions of them.'

But they weren't jewels. They were something even more beautiful.

As the children approached the hill they heard a low, high-pitched rustling; a soft vibrating hum that trembled the air. Then, to their amazement, the blaze of colour began to move: shimmering: palpitating: rising and falling, as the butterflies opened and shut their wings. Suddenly, like bees, they swarmed – disturbed by the children's approach – and in a great rainbow-tinted cloud went swirling south: south for the Victorian plains.

The hill lost its magic. The sun streamed down. The children plodded on.

At midday they rested for a couple of hours in the shade of a steep-sided ravine. Here they ate the last of the yabbies. To both of them, the prawn-like creatures tasted vaguely salt. And they had no water. The girl dozed, drugged to immobility by the heat of the sun: but the boy was restless. Soon he got to his feet.

'Come on, Mary,' he urged. '*Kurura.* Maybe that valley's over the next hill.'

But it wasn't. Nor over the next. Nor the next. Nor even the one after that, which they reached in the golden sunset.

They camped for the night beneath a low shelf of granite. They were hungry and thirsty; exhausted and disillusioned. There was no wood for a fire, no water for a drink. The sunset wind was cold; and so, when they came out, were the stars: cold and uncaring: cold and uncaring and very far away.

Before they slept the children talked awhile in whispers.

'Pete!' The girl's voice was anxious. 'You think we oughta head back tomorrow? Back for the waterhole?'

'Course not!' The little boy was scornful. 'The darkie said there's water over the hills. We'll go on.'

CHAPTER SIXTEEN

D AWN brought wreaths of mist, as the heat of the sun warmed the dew-wet rocks, making them steam like tarmac after summer rain. The children woke damp and cold, hungry and thirsty, their mouths dry and their voices hoarse.

'Come on, Mary,' Peter's croak was harsh as a kookaburra's. 'I don't like this place. Let's push on.'

He led off, round a shoulder of smooth-grained granite. Both children moved a deal more slowly than the day before. Every step required a conscious effort.

They found that the shoulder joined on to a solid massif, a great wedge-like block of hills flanked by a subsidiary ridge which ran directly across their line of advance. Atop this ridge little puffs of cloud, sun-tinted fawn and pink, were rising and falling to the breath of unseen air draughts. Mary looked at the clouds: thoughtfully: hopefully. She tried to remember her geography lessons – in hot climates weren't clouds supposed to form over water? Maybe beyond the ridge they'd come at last to the longed-for valley. She said nothing to Peter – disillusion, if it came, would be too cruel – but somehow her eagerness communicated itself to the little boy; he quickened his stride.

But the ridge proved unexpectedly steep, especially

its last hundred feet. Here the rock was smooth, devoid of vegetation, swept clean by wind, scorched bare by sun. Toe-holds and foot-holds were hard to find.

'Careful, Pete.' Mary paused, wiped the sweat out of her eyes and pointed to the left. 'Over there. It's not so steep.'

Slowly, painfully, they inched their way higher.

The clouds had changed colour now, changed from pink and fawn to a dazzling white. Like puffs of cotton wool in a sky of Reckitt's blue, they bobbed and curtsied along the farther slope of the ridge, almost within the children's hand grasp. And below them Mary could see more cloud: strato-cumulus: layer upon layer. Her hopes rose.

'Careful near the top, Pete. T'other side may be a cliff.'

They reached the crest together – the longed-for crest, swept by a cool, moisture-laden wind – and stood, hand in hand, looking down on the valley-of-waters-under-the-earth.

They couldn't see much detail in the valley itself, for it was blanketed in cloud, but the general layout was clear. It was a rift valley, steep-sided, about three miles wide, splitting the hills like an axe-cut. Through occasional breaks in the cloud the children could see belts of woodland and the distant gleam of water.

Peter danced on the crest of the ridge.

'Just like the darkie told us, Mary. Food and water. *Yeemara* and *arkooloola*.'

The girl nodded.

For a moment the clouds drifted away, revealing a broad, slow-moving ribbon of water, reed-lined, dotted with water-birds, and beautiful as the river that ran out of Eden. Then the layers of strato-cumulus closed up. But the children had seen their vision: knew they'd been led to the promised land. Hand in hand they scrambled and slithered into the valley-of-waters-under-the-earth.

CHAPTER SEVENTEEN

THE girl lay on her side, propped up on one elbow, cutting the fourteenth notch into a branch of yacca. The boy watched her.

'How long you reckon we been here, Mary?'

She counted the notches, first those on one side, then those on the other.

'Eight days in the desert. Six in the valley.'

It seemed to both of them far longer. The past, especially to the boy, was like another world.

They lay beside a shallow lagoon, both of them naked – for on their third day in the valley the girl's dress had been torn beyond repair by the claws of a koala. In front of them the reed-fringed water, motionless as glass, went looping away down-valley; behind them the hills towered up, their summits wreathed in cloud; on either side of them the virgin forests, dark as a cathedral vault, sprawled almost to the water's edge. It was midday, and the valley-of-waters-under-the-earth lay motionless, asleep in the heat of the sun.

For six days the children had wandered slowly up-valley, exploring the curving lagoons, the reedy marshlands and the belts of semi-tropical forest. They had found a number of animals, fish, and reptiles; and a great multitude of birds; but of human beings there was never a sign. They had had plenty to drink and plenty to eat – not always what they'd have chosen (for the water duck eluded their every trap and snare) – but at least something: fruit or vegetable, reptile or fish. Now they had come to an especially beautiful reach of the valley, and the girl – much to her brother's disgust – was preparing to make a home – 'just a hut of reeds,' she had said, 'in case we want to come back.' Peter had jibed at the idea of home-making. 'Gee, Mary,' he'd said, 'what we wanna house for? If it rains, we can shelter in the forest.' But the girl had seemed so disappointed, that he'd agreed to call a halt until the reed-home was made.

He wasn't, in one way, the least bit sorry to have an excuse to rest; to lie back in the lush, sun-hot grass and assimilate all that had happened in the last few days. They had seen such wonderful things; especially since they had come to the valley....

*

They had gone first to the lagoons: to the chain of looping billabongs, fed by underground springs, that lay like a string of sapphires spilt into the hollow of the valley. At first they'd had eyes for nothing but the water: the clear-blue, longed-for water, that in a few wonderful moments took the harshness out of their voices, the aching out of their throats, and the fear out of their hearts.

Then they had noticed the birds.

They were everywhere: in water and reeds, trees and sky; and they were quite fearless. The children stared at them, wandered among them, watched and observed them with a wonderment that increased with every hour of every day.

They saw the wood-ducks; the ducks that nest in trees; that carry their young to water by the scruff of their necks, as a cat carries her kittens. They saw the tail-less swamp coots, nibbling wild celery as they floated by on self-made rafts. They saw the snake-birds, with their long rubbery necks and pointed-dagger bills. And the jacaras – the legendary Jesus-birds – walking the water on their long, dispropor-tionate toes (that use the fragile underwater lily-leaves as stepping-stones). They saw dabchicks and zebra-ducks: marsh-bitterns and pelicans. And late one evening they saw the dance of the brolgas.

They were looking for a place to camp when Peter saw them: a cluster of eight or nine long-billed, stalk-like birds, slim, silver-grey, and elegant, standing one-legged on the water's edge. As the children watched them they saw no sign; but suddenly – as if at a clearly understood command – the brolgas came to life, moved gracefully into a circle. One bird took up position in the centre. He was the leader: the leader of the ritual dance. Opening wide his wings, he began a stately pirouette, a slow-motion quadrille. The others followed his lead; in stylized step they pranced solemnly around the circle, their feet moving in per-fect time, their wings rising and falling to the beat of unheard music. The dance went on for several minutes – more than five, less than ten – then, quite suddenly, it ended. As if at another command the brolgas broke circle, moved into a random cluster, and took up their original one-legged stance gazing peacefully across the lagoon. The children passed within six feet of them, but they never turned their heads.

And the birds of the forest were as strange and wonderful as the birds of the lagoons.

The children never tired of watching them. They saw the mistletoe birds planting their crops: plastering tree trunks with the reeds of the parasites that would later provide them with food. They saw the hawks fanning their nests, bringing their eggs to the requisite temperature for hatching; the butcher-birds stocking their larders, impaling live beetles, moths, and fledgelings on the thorns of the iron-bark; and the rifle-birds, gilding their basin-like nests with the cast-off skins of snakes.

Every sunrise and every sunset the bird songs were near-deafening: a diurnal cacophony of notes clear and limpid, bizarre and unmelodious. The soft cadences of pilot-birds, the wolf-wail of soldiers; the croon of yellow-bellies and the sandpapery scour of scissor-grinders. While at night even stranger sounds echoed among the moon-white trees. The cow-like moo of the bittern, the yap of the barking owl, the coo-ee of the brain-fever bird, and rising above them all the nightmarish scream of the channel-bill: a maniacal shriek which terrified the water rodents into scurrying flight, making them betray their presence to the hovering bird.

No less wonderful than the birds were the trees of the forest with their parasitic flowers and vines.

The children had been a little afraid of the forest at

first; it was so enormous; so dark and earthy-smelling, with tree trunks soaring skyward, and strange, evilly-fashioned plants choking each other to death in a slime of decomposing vegetation. To start with they had stayed on its edges, among maiden-blush of reddish brown and heartswood of emerald green. Then, becoming bolder, they ventured a little way in: to where sycamore vied with tulip-wood, and the cassias dug their quinine-producing roots deep into the fertile soil. And at last they dared the centre: the heart of the primeval wonderland.

Here they found a fantastic battleground of tree and creeper, parasite and vine; with the bodies of the vanquished decomposing in the humid soil. The trees soared skyward, slim and straight, seeking the life-giving sun. But around them, choking them to death, coiled the dodders – the predatory vines, sucking the nutriment out of their roots, gripping the trees with tentacles like tightening tourniquets. And intertwined with the dodders were the jikkas: headless, tail-less, rootless, vegetable snakes; growing on and on, from either end, wrapping their vampire arms around anything they touched.

But, as the children were quick to see, even such a charnel-house as the forest centre was not devoid of beauty – the staghorns, their leaves rearing skyward like the antlers of mating deer; the rock lilies, their bells as white as virgin snow; and the orchids, dangling like gossamer clouds out of the dark trees. They wandered through twisting tunnels, arcaded with vegetation through which the sun had never penetrated; they smelt the rich humid soil which had never felt the stir of a drying wind. At first they were filled with awe and amazement, but eventually, after three or four days of exploration, they became as much at home in the forest as they had been in the desert.

Together they watched the ant-lion lying in wait for his prey, lurking at the base of his self-dug trap, waiting for a victim to come plunging in to his death. Together they watched the fisherman-spider, lowering his single thread baited with sweet-scented adhesive saliva; then when the bait was taken, hauling the thread in, hand over hand. They saw the stick-like praying-mantis, the blue-skinned, red-capped cassowary, and – on their third day in the valley – they saw the koala.

They were on the fringe of the forest, collecting hips from the bush-roses which grew in banks among the eucalyptus trees, the day Mary lost her dress.

'Look!'

She pointed to one of the trees. Half-way down its smooth-grained trunk was a moving ball of silver-grey: a koala, shifting from tree to tree, from one supply of gum leaves to the next. Quietly the children crept to the foot of the eucalyptus. Slowly, steadily, one leg at a time, the koala descended.

It was a mother koala, and clinging to its back was a cub: a harmless, fist-sized teddy bear: fat, tufted-eared, button-eyed, and covered in smooth sheening fur.

When the bears were about three feet from the

ground, Peter darted suddenly round the trunk. He grabbed the cub by the scruff of its neck, jerked it off its mother's back, and thrust it into Mary's arms.

'Bet you never had a doll as nice as that!' he grinned.

The mother bear was far too slow-witted to defend her offspring. But she didn't run away. She hung on to the eucalyptus, blinking her eyes in surprise. Then she started to moan: a low, pathetic, sobbing moan.

Mary's heart went out to her.

'Peter, you beast! She wants her baby.'

She tried to hand the cub back; but its tiny claws were hooked tight on to her dress. The thin material, already rent and worn, gave way. There was a long ripping tear. The dress slid to her feet. The koala sobbed and moaned.

A week ago nothing more calamitous could have happened to the girl. But now, after her initial shock, she felt strangely unembarrassed: more concerned with the cub than with her nakedness. Kicking the remnants of her dress aside, she bent down and very gently returned the baby to its mother's back. Instantly the sobbing ceased. The mother koala looked round, blinked her eyes, licked her cub, climbed down the last three feet of trunk, and waddled off to another eucalyptus.

'Poor thing!' Mary said. 'You oughta known better, Pete.'

*
116

When, after a fashion, the reed hut had been completed, the children moved on. Mary would have been happy to stay; but Peter was eager to explore the rest of the valley.

That evening they came to a bend in the lagoon, and rounding this, saw ahead of them the valley-end: a sheer precipice of granite, and at its base a dark tunnel out of which an underground river flowed in a smooth pouring torrent. About a mile from the end of the valley the river broadened out, forming a shallow reed-fringed lake, three-quarters of a mile across.

Here the children made camp beside the water's edge. They camped early, close to a patch of pink-tinted pipe-clay, agreeing to explore the precipice the following morning. Well before sundown they were eating rose hips and bauble nuts beside a blazing fire.

Then Peter discovered the clay. Discovered that, when moistened, it could be used for drawing; for drawing faces on the smooth lakeside rocks. He called Mary, and together brother and sister experimented with pieces of moistened clay. They found that it drew like chalk on a blackboard; and soon the lakeside rocks were covered with drawings: crude but evocative drawings: drawings that would have been a psychologist's delight.

After a few experimental dabs and smudges, the children settled down to their respective works of art. Peter drew koalas, lizards, and Jesus-birds: symbols of the new life. But Mary drew girls' faces framed with glamorous hair styles, dress designs that might have come out of *Vogue*, and strings of jewels like the

Fifth Avenue advertisements: symbols of the life that was past. And after a while she drew something else: something even more revealing: a house. A simple outline: one door; one window; one chimney; one pathway lined with flowers. Symbol of subconscious hopes and nightly dreams.

The sun dipped under the rim of the hills. The children left their drawings; they stretched out, side by side, in front of the fire. Darkness on velvet wings came flooding into the valley.

'Coo-ee, coo-ee!' sang the brain-fever bird. Over and over again.

Down by the lake a bittern moo-ed among the reeds. A crescent moon lifted clear of the hills. The valley slept.

*

Next morning they smoothed out the ash of their fire. They were just starting off to explore the head of the valley when they saw the smoke. A thin spiral of wood-smoke, pencilling the skyline above the opposite shore of the lake.

CHAPTER EIGHTEEN

THE smoke rose lazily: a slender, blue-grey column, pencil straight. For a long time the children looked at it in silence.

Suddenly the column broke, changed to a succession of puffs: in sequences of three; one large, one medium, one small.

'They're signalling, Pete.'

'Yes.'

The boy looked first at the smoke then at his sister; he saw that her eyes were shining, her lips parted. In the ashes he traced a pattern with the toe of his foot.

'You reckon we oughta answer?'

She nodded, silently, with eyes for nothing but the smoke.

They raked over the ash, pushed in kindling wood, and soon there rose from beside the bed of pipe-clay an answering column of bluish-grey, a misty spear stabbing the azure sky.

'Fetch a branch, Mary. A big 'un, with lots of leaves.'

The girl knew what was wanted: something light enough to lift, but bulky enough to block off the smoke. Soon their column too was broken into a sequence of irregular puffs.

While the boy signalled, the girl watched; watched the farther shore of the lake. Suddenly she saw movement. She strained her eyes; but the figures she had momentarily caught sight of merged chameleon-like into the background of lush-growing reeds. For a while everything was very still. Then the figures appeared again; three ill-defined pin-points leaving the column of wood-smoke, coming down to the lagoon. The sunlight glinted on three fountains of spray, as the strangers dived into the lake. A second later three arrow-heads of white were moving slowly towards them across the sunlit water.

'They're coming, Pete.'

The boy left the fire. Came and stood by his sister. Saw she was trembling. Took her hand.

'Don't worry, Mary. I'll look after you.'

She squeezed his hand: gratefully.

'You reckon they're white men, Pete? Or black, like the darkie?'

The children strained their eyes as the swimmers came steadily nearer. They swam in single file; and it seemed to Peter that their heads were black and abnormally large.

'I reckon they're darkies, Mary. Darkies with big heads!'

The girl nodded; she'd come to the same conclusion herself. She had expected to be terrified at the thought of herself being naked and the strangers being black; yet now that the fact of their blackness had to be faced up to, she realized – unexpectedly – that she wasn't nearly as frightened as if they'd been white!

Holding Peter's hand, she stood at the edge of the water, waiting.

The swimmers came splashing into the shallows. Now that they were nearer, the children could solve the mystery of the size of their heads: they were carrying bundles.

The first swimmer was a full-grown male; and perched athwart his shoulders was a piccaninny, a baby three-year-old, his fingers clutching his father's hair.

The second swimmer was an adult female: a smiling, broad-faced gin. Her bundle was a young *warrigal*: a half-grown dingo pup, its body draped round the back of her neck.

The third and last swimmer was a young lubra, round about Mary's age; strapped to the top of her head was a yam-laden dilly-bag.

The man grounded his feet. He waded out of the water and set the piccaninny down. He was a tall man: straight as a lath: sinuous from head to toe. His hair was straight and jet black, his chest was cicatrized with a V-shaped, shoulder-to-shoulder weal, and he was quite naked. The women followed him, the water glistening on their skin like black pearls. The gin was well-formed, almost buxom; the girl, like Mary, slim, supple, and lithe.

The man's eyes were curious. He addressed himself to Peter.

'Worum gala?'

His voice was deep, yet strangely soft and lilting; like the bush boy's, only several octaves lower.

While Peter floundered into conversation, the women turned their attention to Mary.

Deeds speak louder than words; and the young black girl and the white quickly came to an understanding. The lubra opened up her dilly-bag, and offered Mary a yam. The gift was accepted, and a handful of bauble nuts offered in return. The gin nodded and smiled, and a few moments later understanding turned to something deeper, when the piccaninny – realizing he had missed a share-out of food – started to cry, and Mary picked him up. He stopped instantly, and started to play with her hair: with her long golden hair that hung almost down to her waist.

And as the piccaninny cemented friendship between white girl and black, so the warrigal – the dingo pup – served as a link between man and boy. For Peter loved dogs. The warrigal reminded him of his basenji way back in Charleston. He listened to the black-fellow man with only half his attention; his eyes were on the dog. Suddenly, unexpectedly, he went scampering off – the sight of the warrigal worrying a sycamore branch was too great a temptation. In a moment boy and dog were joined in playful combat, splashing together in clouds of spray through the shallows of the lagoon.

For a moment the black-fellow man blinked in surprise. Then he laughed. He saw that the women-folk were happily sharing food, and lay down among the rocks.

After a while he saw the children's drawings.

He looked at them casually at first, noting the crude inaccuracies of Peter's koalas and lizards; then his eyes passed to the girl's pictures. He sat up then, intrigued. He squinted at the hair styles, seeking in them some clue as to the strangers' race or tribe. He got up and walked slowly down the line of drawings, peering closely at each. And at last, at the very end, he came to the house: to Mary's dream house: one door; one window; one chimney; one pathway lined with flowers.

'Awhee! Awhee!'

He sucked in his lips.

The gin came across; quickly; and together they peered at the dream house. After a while Mary, still carrying the piccaninny, joined them. They looked first at her then at the house.

'Awhee! Awhee!'

The gin's voice was filled with curiosity, almost with awe. She spoke quickly, excitedly, pointing first to the dream house then to the hills on the far side of the valley. Quite suddenly Mary got the gist of what she was saying. Hope surged within her. Over the hills was a house. Not just a hut such as natives lived in, but a house like the one she had drawn: a white man's house: a first stepping-stone on the long, long trail that would, one wonderful and longed-for day, lead them back to home.

'Where? Oh, where?'

Her eagerness was something the Aboriginals could understand.

The black man's eyes were sympathetic. Gently

he took the girl by the hand and led her down to the sand beside the lagoon.

Peter, seeing them talking so earnestly, left the *warrigal* and came and stood beside his sister.

He saw the black man point first to a valley looping aslant the hills like a tired snake. The black man mimed the climb of the valley: his feet rising, his knees sagging. At the top he indicated that the children should sleep. He lay down on the sand and snored. The gin giggled. Then, with the point of a yacca branch, he traced a line heading east, into the rising sun. After a while the line broke, and with a couple of curves the black man indicated a hill. Then, beyond the hill, the line went on. Soon came another, lower hill; and here, the black man indicated, there was water; he drew a circle, pointed to the lagoon, and lapped like a dog. He also indicated food: yams: he drew them beside the hill and champed his teeth. And here too he indicated sleep: again the lying down, again the snoring. The children nodded. Next day the line continued east, towards another, higher hill. And here, at the base of the hill, it stopped. Ended at a house. The black man drew it: one door; one window; one chimney; one pathway lined with flowers.

The children looked at each other. The girl's eyes were like the stars of the Southern Cross.

'Oh, Pete!'

She burst suddenly into tears.

Peter looked at the *warrigal* and the reeds and the red-gums and the glistening expanse of the lagoon, and knew in that moment that every detail of what he'd seen in the last two weeks he'd remember for the rest of his life. Then he walked slowly across to the fire and collected the last of their bauble nuts. He stood for a moment looking not at the others but up and down the sun-drenched valley; then he went across to the black-fellow man and held out his hand.

'Good-bye!' he said very formally.

The black man grinned and he too held out his hand.

Peter turned to the girl.

'Come on, Mary,' he said. '*Kurura.*'

He led the way along the shore of the lake.

OTHER NEW YORK REVIEW CLASSICS*

* *For a complete list of titles, visit www.nyrb.com or write to:
Catalog Requests, NYRB, 435 Hudson Street, New York, NY 10014*